Deadly Backfire

Clint knew to keep his guns in proper working order under most any circumstances. Fortunate for him. Quite the opposite for the men behind him . . .

Clint twisted in the saddle while bringing the rifle up to his shoulder in a smooth motion. After taking quick aim, he fired off a round that rocked one of the men back in his saddle. Before any of the others even knew their friend had been hit, Clint had worked the rifle's lever and was taking another shot.

Just as the first one to be hit was struggling to sit upright and not be thrown from his horse, another of the three riders caught some of Clint's lead. The second one wasn't as fortunate as the first and felt a powerful kick square in his chest.

With his arms and legs splayed to the sides, the second rider was pitched into the air. Then he landed on his back in the dirt behind all the horses. His fists clawed at the ground while his legs thrashed, but he gave up the ghost a few seconds later . . .

297

DANGEROUS CARGO

J. R. ROBERTS

JOVE BOOKS, NEW YORK

THE BERKLEY PUBLISHING GROUP
Published by the Penguin Group
Penguin Group (USA) Inc.
375 Hudson Street, New York, New York 10014, USA
Penguin Group (Canada), 90 Eglinton Avenue East, Suite 700, Toronto, Ontario M4P 2Y3, Canada
(a division of Pearson Penguin Canada Inc.)
Penguin Books Ltd., 80 Strand, London WC2R 0RL, England
Penguin Group Ireland, 25 St. Stephen's Green, Dublin 2, Ireland (a division of Penguin Books Ltd.)
Penguin Group (Australia), 250 Camberwell Road, Camberwell, Victoria 3124, Australia
(a division of Pearson Australia Group Pty. Ltd.)
Penguin Books India Pvt. Ltd., 11 Community Centre, Panchsheel Park, New Delhi—110 017, India
Penguin Group (NZ), Cnr. Airborne and Rosedale Roads, Albany, Auckland 1310, New Zealand
(a division of Pearson New Zealand Ltd.)
Penguin Books (South Africa) (Pty.) Ltd., 24 Sturdee Avenue, Rosebank, Johannesburg 2196,
South Africa

Penguin Books Ltd., Registered Offices: 80 Strand, London WC2R 0RL, England

This is a work of fiction. Names, characters, places, and incidents either are the product of the author's imagination or are used fictitiously, and any resemblance to actual persons, living or dead, business establishments, events, or locales is entirely coincidental.

DANGEROUS CARGO

A Jove Book / published by arrangement with the author

PRINTING HISTORY
Jove edition / September 2006

Copyright © 2006 by Robert J. Randisi.

ISBN: 0-515-14202-6

JOVE®
Jove Books are published by The Berkley Publishing Group,
a division of Penguin Group (USA) Inc.,
375 Hudson Street, New York, New York 10014.
JOVE is a registered trademark of Penguin Group (USA) Inc.
The "J" design is a trademark belonging to Penguin Group (USA) Inc.

PRINTED IN THE UNITED STATES OF AMERICA

10   9   8   7   6   5   4   3   2   1

ONE

As Clint rode through New Mexico and into Nevada, the scenery around him changed as if Mother Nature couldn't make up her mind. One day he was surrounded by desert and patches of dry shrubs, and the next he was treated to the sight of mountains on the horizon. Although he'd seen those sights before, Clint wouldn't have minded taking them in once more.

Unfortunately, he didn't have that kind of time to waste.

For the last few days, he'd been pushing Eclipse to his limit. The Darley Arabian stallion was always up for a good run, but over the last few hours, he'd been showing the first signs of slowing down. He still responded to every one of Clint's commands, but his steps were getting heavier and his breaths were churning out of him like steam from an engine.

"Come on, boy," Clint urged over the thunder of Eclipse's hooves against the dirt. "Just a little further."

Even though Eclipse kept tearing across the landscape, his head wobbled a bit as if to let Clint know he didn't believe a word that had just come from his mouth.

Clint couldn't blame the stallion if he did doubt those last few words. There was still a ways to go before either of them could rest and most of that land was harsh, unforgiving slopes of rock.

It was all Clint could do to keep hold of the reins without dropping from the saddle. Though he could anticipate nearly every shift the stallion made a few seconds ahead of time, the land beneath Eclipse's hooves wasn't half as predictable.

Flat ground could be just that, or it could be a steep incline covered by a smoothed-over layer of sandy dirt. The bushes a couple yards ahead might conceal a cluster of low rocks or it might break into pieces at the next stiff breeze. So far, Eclipse was doing a hell of a job navigating the terrain, leaving Clint to hold on and pray for mercy.

Before too much longer, Clint squinted to the horizon in front of him and studied every bump he could see. When he finished, he let out a breath and pulled back on the reins.

"Whoa. Looks like we can take it easy for a stretch."

Eclipse slowed to a quick walk. His chest was heaving a bit and his breaths roared loudly from his nostrils. He was still a young horse, however, and regained his second wind easily enough.

Twisting in the saddle, Clint looked behind him until he found himself glancing a bit too close to the sun. He blinked away a few spots, rubbed his eyes, and then took his canteen from where it hung from his saddle. The lukewarm water felt damn good splashing against the back of his throat.

Cupping his hand and filling it as best he could, he offered a drink to the Darley Arabian. Eclipse turned his head after catching sight of the water and drank from Clint's hand. The horse was straining, but lapped up what he could in a matter of seconds.

"Think that'll hold you for a while?" Clint asked. When he pulled back an empty hand, he said, "Guess not. Here's a bit more."

Eclipse wet his whistle a little longer and then shook

some of the dust from his mane. That brief respite seemed to be enough to put back the steam in his stride.

Clint slung the canteen back over the saddle and immediately stuck his hand into one of the pouches hanging over Eclipse's back. His palm had no trouble finding the leather bundle he was after, which allowed him to let out the breath that had gathered in his lungs. As much as he liked the scenery, he would have hated to go back and retrace his steps through miles of flat, brown land in search of a flat, brown package.

"There's supposed to be a town not too far from here," Clint said under his breath. "If Jake got his signals crossed about that, I'll just have to ride back into Lincoln County and shove this package . . ."

Clint didn't need to finish his sentence. Or, more likely, he wasn't able to finish it since he was suddenly distracted by a shot which cracked through the air behind him. The bullet whipped over his head with plenty of room to spare, but he wasn't of a mind to stick around so the men behind him could improve their aim.

"All right, boy," Clint said while snapping his reins. "Looks like our rest is over."

Eclipse's response was a subtle whinny before digging his hooves into the dirt and racing forward. Before the reins were snapped a second time, the Darley Arabian was building up to full speed.

Clint hunkered down over Eclipse's back so he could easily shift back and forth in the saddle. It also gave him some peace of mind as more and more shots hissed toward him. When he shot a glance over his shoulder, Clint made out three shapes charging straight for him. They were coming at him from the same direction as the sun, which explained how they'd gotten so close.

Clint's first impulse was to get moving as quickly as the stallion's legs could carry them. It didn't take long, however, for him to be reminded of how tired Eclipse was after all the running he'd already done. The Darley Arabian would run until he fell over if Clint asked him to, but Clint wasn't eager to put the stallion through that kind of hell.

Instead, Clint eased back just enough on the reins to allow the riders behind him to move in a little closer. In a matter of seconds, he could hear the men hollering back and forth to each other as if they'd already won the fight. Clint just smirked at that and shook his head.

Some men were just too stupid to know when they were outmatched.

Reaching down with one hand, Clint eased the rifle from where it was stored on his saddle. He wrapped the reins around one hand while levering in a round and taking a quick look into the rifle's loading mechanism. Sand and grit could go a long ways in mucking up a weapon's inner workings. Fortunately, Clint knew to keep his guns in proper working order under most any circumstances.

Fortunate for him, anyway.

Quite the opposite for the men behind him.

Relying on his ears more than anything else, Clint waited until the riders behind him had gotten a little closer. The shots were coming faster and they were buzzing closer to him as they passed by. Once he knew the other men were in just the right spot, Clint made his move.

Clint twisted in the saddle while bringing the rifle up to his shoulder in a smooth motion. After taking quick aim, he fired off a round that rocked one of the other men back in his saddle. Before any of the others even knew their friend had been hit, Clint had worked the rifle's lever and was taking another shot.

Just as the first one to be hit was struggling to sit upright and not be thrown from his horse, another of the three riders caught some of Clint's lead. The second one wasn't as fortunate as the first and felt a powerful kick square in his chest.

With his arms and legs splayed to the sides, the second

rider was pitched into the air. Then he landed on his back in the dirt behind all the horses. His fists clawed at the ground while his legs thrashed, but he gave up the ghost a few seconds later.

Clint was still sighting along the rifle's barrel as that horseman dropped. Another round was ready to be fired, but he waited to see what the others would do. For the moment, the remaining two riders were trying to figure out where they'd lost their partner. Once they spotted the body, they weren't so anxious to keep firing.

Nodding to himself, Clint straightened up in the saddle and touched his heels to Eclipse's sides. The Darley Arabian took off like a shot, leaving the other two riders in his dust.

TWO

Eclipse only had to ride at full speed for a few minutes. After that, he'd already put enough space between himself and the other two riders that Clint could breathe a whole lot easier. Once more, he pulled back on the reins and took a look around. Although he didn't see anyone right away, Clint didn't allow himself to relax.

"I'd say those fellows were rattled enough to give us some breathing room," Clint said as a way to clear some of the air from his lungs. "Hopefully, they'll be smart enough to let us ride the rest of the way without being bothered."

Even though he was just thinking out loud, Clint had an easier time believing that Eclipse could understand English than what he was actually saying. The riders had been dogging his trail for a whole lot longer than this one day and there was no reason for Clint to think they'd stop now.

It did do him some good when the sun shifted in the sky enough for him to get his first glimpse of the buildings in the distance. "Now that is a sight for sore eyes," he said.

The town wavered like a mirage as waves of heat and dust churned through the air. It wasn't a big town, but it was bigger than plenty of settlements that Clint had found scattered throughout the desert. Of course, this place wasn't exactly in the desert.

The terrain had shifted yet again, exchanging flat ground for tall rocks jutting up in a series of squared angles that resembled a stack of hat boxes arranged with the smallest one on top. Compared to the mountains in the distance, those rocks looked more like something someone had built than a natural formation.

To some, those rocks might have been beautiful.

When Clint looked at them, he couldn't help but wince.

The rocks were colored in all shades of brown and red, topped with trees that were too tough to wilt in the direct sunlight. It was those very rocks that made the ride so dangerous. They were such an ideal spot for an ambush that they might have been built by overly anxious bandits. Gunmen strong enough to climb to the top of the flat rocks could stretch out with their rifles and pick off anything that moved beneath them.

Instinctively, Clint reloaded his rifle and kept it propped against his hip as he rode toward the rocks. As much as he would have liked to shave a few hours off his trip by riding through a pass that cut through the rocks, he preferred only having to watch one side rather than two.

Before too long, Eclipse found himself climbing up a steep incline that was made even more treacherous by the shifting gravel beneath his hooves. The Darley Arabian kept his balance and kept moving, however, while Clint watched for trouble from the saddle.

He didn't have to wait long, since a man's head soon poked over the side of one of the taller rocks. A crisp whistle cut through the air and was soon followed by the sight of other heads poking up to get a look at Eclipse.

When Clint saw those heads, he thought of a row of clay targets snapping up in a shooting gallery. He fought back the impulse to crack every last one of those targets and simply brought his rifle around so that it was in plain sight.

The men on those rocks were too confident to do more than twitch at the sight of the rifle. They responded by showing their own guns and then shouting down at Clint.

"Toss what you're carrying and turn back," came a voice from the top of the rocks. "Otherwise, we'll burn you down."

Clint kept riding slowly around the rocks. In the time it had taken for the other man to shout his threat, Clint had already surveyed his situation and come up with a few ways to handle it. "How do I know you won't shoot me even if I do give it up?" he asked.

"You don't, but you can be sure we'll kill you if you don't give it up."

After making a show of thinking it over for a few seconds, Clint shook his head. "Nah. I made it this far, so if it's all the same to you, I'll just keep going."

There was a moment of silence when Clint could feel the stunned glances that were coming down at him from those rocks. After he could calm himself enough to talk, the spokesman up there said, "It ain't the same to me! Toss that package right now, goddammit!"

Clint took a deep breath and tightened his grip on his rifle. "When this is over," he muttered to Eclipse, "remind me to find Jake and have a good, long talk with him. Either that, or you could just kick him in the ass for me and be done with it . . ."

THREE

A few days earlier, Clint had been sitting in a New Mexico saloon, playing cards with two scruffy cowboys, a snake-oil salesman, and a twitchy fellow by the name of Jake McKean. Although that sounded like the start of a bad joke, it was all too real. In fact, Clint was in a joking mood right up until one of those cowboys threw his drink into Jake's face and pushed himself back from the table.

"What the hell did you just say?" the cowboy snarled as he jumped to his feet.

Jake was a skinny fellow with the narrow build of a professional rider. He also had the twitchy eyes that not only marked him as someone who was used to being on the move, but made it real easy for Clint to tell when he was holding something better than two pair.

"No need to get your feathers ruffled," Jake said as he put on a shaky grin and held out both hands. "It ain't that I don't have the money at all. It's just that I don't have it right here with me."

The cowboy was in his late twenties and smelled as if he'd sat down to play cards before even tossing a sideways glance at a bathtub. He looked over to his partner as though he was waiting for a translation. "What the hell's the difference?" he grunted before too long. "You made a bet. You lost and now you don't wanna pay. That's all there is to it."

"I can get the money," Jake insisted. "I just need to get to my horse."

Although the cowboy's draw wasn't especially quick or steady, it was good enough for him to get his hand wrapped around his gun before Jake could do much about it. Staring over the barrel of his rusted Smith & Wesson, the cowboy said, "You must think I'm a damn fool if you think I'm gonna let you get anywhere near that horse."

Up to now, Clint had been content to let the two men settle their own differences. As soon as the iron had cleared leather, however, he knew he had to put his nose in where at least one man didn't want it. He eased back from the table just enough for the modified Colt to be seen.

"Take it easy," Clint said. "There's no reason for anyone to get hurt."

"That's easy for you to say," the cowboy grunted. "You ain't the one that's been cheated."

"Cheated?" Jake sputtered. "I lost!"

"That's right, you did! So pay up!"

"I told you. I just need to—"

Already sensing where the conversation was headed, Clint interrupted by saying, "He needs to get to his horse and you don't want him there. At this rate, we won't get anywhere and I'd like to get back to the game. Why don't we just settle this and get on with things?"

"And how would you propose we do that?" the cowboy asked.

"Simple. I go out to his horse and get what he needs."

Both of the other men thought about that suggestion for a moment. Although the cowboy was wary, Jake seemed to take to the notion just fine.

"How do I know I can trust you?" the cowboy asked.

Clint chuckled and shrugged. "If we were in on this together, wouldn't we both be winning more?"

Everyone at the table glanced over to the stack of chips in front of Clint's and Jake's chairs. Clint was doing fairly well for himself, but Jake's spot was empty. Shrugging, the other cowboy said, "He's got a point."

"Fine," the first cowboy said after letting out a breath. "But my partner will go along with you. If you try anything he don't like, he'll make you sorry you got tangled up in this."

The threat hit Clint almost as hard as a ball of yarn thrown by a sickly child. "All right, it's a deal." Looking over to Jake, he asked, "Where can I find the money?"

Jake ground his teeth together, but didn't say anything.

"You do have the money, right?" Clint asked.

Slowly, Jake started to nod.

"Then tell me where it is. You did lose a bet and you need to pay up. Either do it now, or take your chances on your own later."

Slouching as if all the wind had been stolen from him, Jake replied, "I keep it in a pouch under my saddle. It's at the back, toward the left."

Clint nodded and got up. "All right, then. We'll go out and get the money. The bet will be paid off and this will be over. Right?"

The cowboy nodded, but was reluctant to take his eyes off of Jake. "So long as I get my money, I'll be happy."

"Good. That's all that matters," Clint said in something of a snide tone.

The cowboy didn't take any notice of what Clint said or how he said it. He was too intent on watching every twitch on Jake's face and tightening his grip around the pistol in his hand.

Clint didn't bother checking to see if the other cowboy was following him. He could hear the younger man's steps plainly enough and would have been able to smell him from several miles away. Since Jake had been talking about his horse throughout most of the game, Clint knew exactly which one of the animals tied up outside the saloon to go to.

Although the spotted mare shifted uncomfortably when Clint started loosening the saddle, she calmed down after a few kind words and pats on the side. The leather of the saddle was so well worn that it seemed to have been melted onto the horse's back. When Clint slipped his fingers underneath it, he had a bit of trouble finding what he was after.

"Son of a bitch," the cowboy grunted when he saw the expression on Clint's face. "That prick was lying. I knew it."

Just then, Clint's fingers found one section of leather that separated from the rest. It was a thin pouch that had been pressed into something like a leather envelope. It was also right where Jake had said it would be. Clint removed the thin pouch and held it up for the cowboy to see. Clint untied the leather straps and took a peek inside.

"All right," Clint said with a grin. "Looks like our game will go on."

The cowboy leaned forward and seemed somewhat disappointed when he spotted the folded bills stuffed into the envelope. "It don't look like enough."

"Let's take one thing at a time, shall we?"

Clint walked back into the saloon with the cowboy trailing behind him. The first cowboy was still in his spot, holding his gun on Jake. By this time, the others inside the saloon had taken notice of the standoff and were waiting in expectant silence for the first shot to be fired.

Tossing the envelope onto the table, Clint said, "Here you go, Jake. Count it up and pay what you owe."

The cowboy with the gun started to reach for the envelope, but was stopped by an iron grip around his wrist. His eyes widened a bit when he saw who'd grabbed him. He hadn't even seen Clint flinch before his hand had snapped out like a snake.

"Let the man pay his debt," Clint said with a warning

glare. "You don't have a claim on any more of the money in that pouch."

The cowboy was reluctant at first, but the hard look in Clint's eyes was enough to show him the light of reason. "All right. Get me my money."

Jake's hands were a bit shaky, but he managed to fish out enough bills to cover his loss. After he handed the money over, he had to sit and stare down the barrel of the cowboy's gun while it was counted. Twice.

"Satisfied?" Jake asked.

The cowboy nodded. "Yeah. I suppose."

"Then how about you put that thing away?"

Still nodding, the cowboy holstered his gun and took his seat. Now that they could tell there wasn't about to be a fight, the rest of the folks in the saloon got back to what they'd been doing in the first place.

The second cowboy dealt the next hand while Clint ordered a round of drinks. Just as things seemed to be headed in the right direction, Jake's eyes lit up and he gleefully made a raise that was triple the size of the pot.

Clint let out a tired groan.

FOUR

After the game, Clint couldn't get out of that saloon fast enough. His stomach was rumbling, so he walked down the street and headed for a place that was run by an old German woman who cooked well enough to tempt the devil himself.

Normally, Clint was friendly with most of the people he played cards with. This time was different, however. Between the frayed tempers of the two cowboys and the reckless way that Jake tossed his money around, Clint had had his fill of the whole lot of them. That was why Clint felt like a rat caught in a trap when he saw Jake come racing over to his table just as a mug of dark beer was set in front of him by the German woman's granddaughter.

"Hey, Clint! Am I glad to see you!"

"It's only been a few minutes, Jake," Clint groaned.

"Yeah, I know. What I meant was that I was hoping to have a word with you, but you got away from me."

"Well, you hunted me down," Clint replied, meaning that phrase very literally. "What's on your mind?"

Jake sat down like he was the guest of honor and almost reached for Clint's beer. He pulled back his hand when he saw the warning glare in Clint's eyes and then frantically waved a hand at the serving girl.

She was a tall blonde who wore her hair in twin braids that hung over both shoulders. Before responding at all to Jake's signal, she caught Clint's eye and waited. He nodded reluctantly at her, which was enough to get her to bring Jake his beer.

"I'm a courier, you see, and—" Jake stopped short to take a sip of his beer. It was the same dark brew that Clint had ordered and instantly twisted his mouth into an ugly grimace. "Jesus Christ, that's bitter. What the hell's wrong with that beer?"

"It's supposed to be that way."

"Really? Oh." Jake took another sip. This time, he concentrated and then nodded approvingly. "Nice! Anyway, I'm a courier by trade and I only meant to stop by here for a short rest."

"There's still enough light to get riding, if you really want to."

Jake laughed, even though there wasn't the first indication on Clint's face to show he was kidding. "All I wanted was a short rest and I got myself into that card game."

"Which almost turned out to be a long rest of the underground variety."

Jake thought about that for a moment and shuddered. "You're right about that. Maybe I would've been better off just riding on into Nevada instead of stopping here."

"Or maybe you could have stuck to making bets that you can afford to lose."

"There's that, too."

Clint took a sip of his beer and savored the rich taste of it. Over the years, a man had to become accustomed to drinking poorly made beer or he would just have to swear off the stuff. Too many saloon owners served up frothy swill for it to be any other way. Clint enjoyed most kinds of beer and could appreciate quality when he found it.

The dark German beer he was drinking was unlike anything he'd ever tasted before. Although it was thick and bitter, there was an aftertaste that left the flavor of honey in his mouth. It was more than enough to put a smile on his face under practically any circumstance.

Seeing that smile, Jake assumed it was meant for him and slapped Clint on the shoulder while lifting his own beer. He drained it as quickly as he could and then slammed the mug down onto the table. "I noticed you carry a gun, sir."

Cringing at the forced formality in Jake's voice, Clint said, "Your eyes are working just fine."

"Since that's the case, I'd like to . . . uh . . . hire your services."

"Plenty of men carry guns, Jake. That doesn't mean they're for hire."

"But some are," Jake said cheerily. "You struck me as one of them."

Clint studied Jake's face and saw nothing but sincerity in his crooked, twitching smile. "Even so, some men might take that as an insult."

After a few seconds, Jake's smile faded and he began to blink nervously. "I didn't mean it like that. Aw, hell. I knew I shouldn't have come here like this."

Although he didn't know exactly why, Clint felt a bit of sympathy for Jake just then. The man had been held at gunpoint and was now struggling just to find the words for what he wanted to say. As a way to alleviate some of that tension, Clint asked, "Why would you need to hire a gun when you carry one of your own?"

Jake didn't even glance at the pistol wedged under his belt. "All my life, I only shot a few snakes and winged one Indian. I'll need more than that if I'm to get where I'm going in one piece."

"And where's that?"

"Hendricks. It's a good-sized town not too far across the border in Nevada. There's a fella there who's waiting for me to deliver a package to him."

"Sounds like your line of work."

"Normally, yes, but this looks to be a dangerous run."

"Didn't you scout it out beforehand?"

"Yes. That's how I know it's going to be a dangerous run."

The footsteps of the approaching server almost covered the sound of Clint's sigh. The smell of the food he'd ordered was enough to take his mind off of the conversation he was having. At least, for a few seconds.

"That looks good," Jake said as he stared at the plate of food the blonde server set down in front of Clint. "Mind if I join you?"

"Actually, there's no need for us to talk about this any longer. I'm not a gun for hire and you get paid to deliver packages. By all accounts, that means you're the one who should take whatever this package is to wherever it needs to go."

"But that was before our card game."

Clint already had a piece of pork on the end of his fork and was dipping it into a pile of mashed potatoes. Before tasting the food, however, he said, "I tried to help you, Jake. If I knew that would be such a problem, I would have let those cowboys shoot you and take all your money."

Jake shook his head quickly. "You're not the problem. It's that those cowboys saw how much money I have that's causing the problem. After you left, I overheard them saying they should bushwhack me after I leave town so they can have the rest."

"Tell the law about it," Clint said through a mouth full of tender pork and tasty potatoes.

"I did. He said he couldn't do much just on account of a rumor."

"That's a wise policy."

"You're right," Jake sighed. "I guess I'll just tuck that money away and ride like the wind. Hopefully, I won't get killed between here and Hendricks."

"This can't be your first tough ride."

"No, but that cowboy still wants to hurt me. I can see it in his eyes."

Clint thought back to all the jokes, taunts, bluffs, and whines that had come out of Jake's mouth during that game and he couldn't exactly blame those cowboys for wanting to do some damage. In fact, the longer Jake stayed at that table, the more Clint wanted to do some damage of his own.

Finally, after a few more bites of food had hit his belly, Clint looked at Jake to find the man wasn't going anywhere. "When are you supposed to ride out of here?" Clint asked.

"Tomorrow, bright and early."

"If you're worried about trouble, I can take a ride with you for a ways. I was about to head out of here myself."

Jake's face brightened and he jumped up from his chair. Doing that, his knees caught the edge of the table, almost sending Clint's plate into his lap. Clint's beer wasn't so fortunate and wound up dumped onto the floor.

"That's great!" Jake said, without seeming to notice the havoc he was causing. "I surely do appreciate this! Are you staying at the Grand?"

"Yeah, but—"

"I'll meet you out front of there tomorrow morning! Thanks so much!" And with that, Jake turned to bolt out the door. He was gone a second later.

Clint leaned back in his chair with his arms out to the sides so he could look down at himself. The front of his shirt was spattered with some gravy and a bit of beer. The rest of his beer had soaked through his pants and was working its way down to his boots.

"Looks like he got both of us," came a voice from Clint's left.

When he turned to take a look, Clint saw the blonde waitress standing with her arms also held out to show the fresh stains on her skirt. She'd only managed to catch a fraction of what Clint got, but the dark beer made a mess out of her tan-colored clothing.

"Does the meal include laundry services?" Clint asked.

FIVE

The blonde server's name was Gretchen, but most everyone called her Greta. She was tall and slender, but had the right kind of hips and breasts to make her body perfectly curved. Her hair was almost always tied into one or two braids with a ribbon at the end, but the most memorable thing about her was her smile.

She even smiled after she'd been splattered by dark beer.

The air hit both of them when they'd walked out of the restaurant, chilling Clint below the waist while sending a shiver up Greta's back. She giggled while leading him across the street to a narrow, two-level house where she and the rest of the restaurant's owners lived. Clint followed her up the stairs and into a bedroom, but he didn't need to be shown where she wanted to go.

After all, it wasn't his first time stepping into that bedroom.

"He got you real good," Greta said with just a hint of a German accent in her voice.

Stepping into the room, Clint walked right into her open arms. "A hell of a lot more than he got you."

The edges of her mouth curled in a tempting way as she

slipped her hands over Clint's chest. "Good thing you left some clothes the last time you were here."

"I'll be quick about changing. I know your grandmother is up and about."

"She's still at the restaurant," Greta said softly. "And she won't leave it unattended."

"So if we're here, she'll stay over there?"

Greta nodded.

"Well then," Clint said while pushing the door shut with the back of his heel, "that's a different story."

Saying that and hearing the door click shut was more than enough to prompt Greta to step forward and wrap her arms around the back of Clint's neck. She was tall enough to look directly into his eyes as she leaned in to press her lips firmly against Clint's mouth.

She tasted like the sweet pastries that she was known to bake and her body was warm to the touch. While he'd been in town, Clint had gotten familiar with the curves of her figure, but he was always willing to do a little more exploring if the opportunity presented itself.

After quickly pulling her blouse from where it was tucked into her skirt, Clint slipped his hands beneath the material so he could feel the soft, smooth flesh underneath. Greta let out a soft little moan as she felt her clothes get peeled away from her body. When Clint's hands found her bare breasts and started to tease her nipples, she leaned her head back as a shiver worked its way through her body.

Suddenly, Greta's eyes snapped open and she fixed Clint with a hungry stare. Keeping her eyes on his, she started to pull the shirt off his back and then began pulling urgently at his belt. By the time she was able to work his pants down, he was fully erect and waiting for her.

"Let's get these off of you," she said while tugging off his boots so she could remove his pants all the way.

As Clint unbuttoned his shirt he said, "Now this is what I call service with a smile."

Greta was on her knees by now and she was smiling widely. She even managed to keep that smile on her face as she opened her mouth and wrapped her lips around the tip of his penis. Slowly, she eased him all the way into her mouth while tightening her lips just enough to get him even harder. Her tongue slid up and down along the shaft of his cock as her head bobbed back and forth.

Clint felt every one of the muscles in his back and shoulders relax as Greta's mouth worked on him. He put one hand on the back of her head so he could guide her momentum while also feeling the smoothness of her hair.

Greta slid her mouth all the way to the end of Clint's penis so the tip was resting on her lower lip. From there, she looked up at him and gave him another naughty smile. Opening her mouth a bit wider, she leaned forward until every last inch of him was swallowed up inside of her.

That feeling made Clint a bit weak in the knees. It was so distracting that at first he didn't even notice the voice calling his name. In fact, he didn't notice it at all until he saw Greta glancing toward the bedroom window.

Taking him out of her mouth so she could wrap her hand around the shaft of his cock, Greta asked, "Did you hear that?"

"No."

"I think it was your name."

Slowly, the blood started flowing above Clint's waist and he was able to hear the voice a little clearer. Sure enough, someone was shouting his name. The bad news was that he immediately recognized the voice.

"Aw, hell," Clint grumbled. "Just ignore it."

"Hey, Clint!" the voice shouted. "You in there?"

Since Greta had already gotten to her feet and was walking toward the bed, Clint hiked up his pants and stomped toward the window. He threw it open hard enough to rattle the glass in its frame.

"What is it, Jake?" Clint growled down to the street.

Jake looked up at him, still wearing the stupid smile on his face that had been there when he'd left the restaurant. "Just wanted to tell you I might be there a bit earlier than we said before. It might be better to start a little before sunup. Is that all right?"

"Yeah, fine."

"You're not a late sleeper?"

"Just go!" Clint snapped. "I said I'd be there and I will. See you tomorrow!"

Without seeming to notice the anger in Clint's voice or the impatience in his eyes, Jake waved up to the window and walked away.

Clint shut the window and turned to find Greta stretched out on the bed. "Now," he said while making his way over to her, "where were we?"

SIX

When she saw Clint walking back to her, Greta stretched her arms over her head and arched her back like a cat that was making itself comfortable on a giant blanket. Her hands wrapped around the slats in the headboard and stayed there as Clint stripped naked and climbed on top of her.

By now, Greta wasn't wearing much of anything. Her blouse was open and hanging off of one shoulder. The skirt was gone, leaving a thin cotton slip which was bunched up and only covering one leg. Her other leg was shapely and covered with a dark stocking held up by a simple garter.

Clint slid his hand up under her slip so he could see her other leg. It was just as shapely as the first and Greta wriggled them slightly the longer Clint kept his hands on them. He managed to peel the slip all the way down so she could kick it away and reveal she wasn't wearing anything else beneath the filmy cotton. Now, Clint was able to let his hands roam freely from the slope of her calves to the buttons connecting the stockings to her garters.

"I love it when you do that," Greta purred.

Clint smirked and tickled the insides of her thighs with his fingertips. "I know you do. Just like I know how much you like it when I do this."

As he said that, Clint dropped down to place his lips against Greta's thigh. Stretching out his arms so he could run his hands along her stomach and beyond, Clint moved slowly over her body while grazing his tongue along her skin.

He started by tasting her leg and then made a straight line between them. The moment his tongue touched her pussy, Greta squirmed and moaned passionately. Clint lingered for just long enough to flick his tongue against her clitoris before moving up along her body. He nibbled a line over her belly, but quickly worked his way to her rounded breasts.

Greta's nipples were pink little nubs that were already erect when Clint's mouth got to them. He placed a few wet kisses on each nipple before moving down a bit and then running his tongue between her breasts and up to her neck. Greta had practically melted into the sheets by the time she felt him take a playful nip at her ear.

Settling in between her legs, Clint could feel the dampness of Greta's vagina against his rigid cock. He reached down and guided himself into her so he could thrust forward with his hips and drive all the way into her. Greta let out a trembling moan as she took him in. Her arms wrapped tightly around him.

After a few thrusts, Greta draped one arm around Clint and grabbed hold of the headboard with the other. She opened her legs wide for him and wriggled her hips in perfect harmony with Clint's. She even knew when to lift them up a bit so Clint could grab hold of her plump backside.

This wasn't the first time that Clint and Greta had shared a bed. Even so, every time seemed to come as a surprise. They never got together with the express intention to roll in the sheets, but that's just what seemed to happen. So far, it had been working out pretty good.

Clint pumped into her once more and drove all the way inside her. From there, he pushed his hips forward a bit more until he saw Greta's eyes open wider and a surprised grin creep onto her face. Then he pulled back and all the way out of her, rolling onto his back.

When he landed on the mattress, Clint said, "I think I'm tired."

"Oh, no you're not!"

Laughing at the insistent way she responded to his comment, Clint pulled Greta closer until she mounted him. Still looking down at him with a scolding expression, Greta took hold of his penis and fitted it between her legs. She then settled down on him and let out a long breath.

She glided on top of him, taking him inside so she could start rocking back and forth. After a few slow movements, she stopped. "Now, I think I am the one who's tired."

Clint merely shook his head, grabbed hold of her hips, and started pumping up into her. He only had to guide her for a few seconds before she began riding him on her own. Her breasts swayed back and forth as she leaned forward and truly got into what she was doing. Her eyes were closed and her face was intent as she rode him with building momentum.

Soon, Greta was breathing harder and her fingers were digging into Clint's shoulders. Clint reached up to cup her breasts in both hands while thrusting into her again and again. He knew when he found the perfect spot because Greta sucked in a quick breath and the lips between her legs tightened around him.

A few more thrusts was all it took before she was trembling with an approaching climax. Clint felt her orgasm pulse through her and kept right on pumping his hips. A few seconds later, he was exploding inside of her.

"Now that," Greta sighed, "is what I call service with a smile."

SEVEN

The sun wasn't anywhere to be seen when Clint dragged himself out of bed. He wouldn't have even gotten out of bed yet if not for the insistent rapping on his door. At first, he'd thought it was rats trapped behind the wall, but rats didn't know him by name.

"Clint," Jake hissed from the hallway outside of Clint's room. "Clint we need to get going."

Clint was no stranger to waking up at or before sunrise. Often, it was a very pleasant time of day. Being dragged out of bed by a strained voice and a constant knocking on his door, however, wasn't pleasant in the least.

After kicking off the sheets and blanket which had been warmed by his own body heat, Clint was greeted by the cold air of his room as he scrambled to find his clothes. He was still thinking about Greta's bedroom, which tricked him into thinking he had much more space in which to get dressed. Because he was in his hotel room, he found himself banging against nearly every surface with a corner on it before he got to the door and pulled it open.

Jake, of course, looked bright and chipper.

"Jesus Christ," Clint grumbled. "I said I was going to meet you, didn't I?"

"You were going to be late."

"How would you know that?"

After making a show of looking Clint up and down, he said, "You were sleeping just now, weren't you?"

"Yeah, but how did . . ." Clint rubbed his eyes and let out a breath. "Never mind. I guess you knew about that the same way you knew where to find me yesterday."

"Oh, you mean across from that restaurant? I just saw you and that serving girl cross the street after I left. Do you know her?"

Clint rolled his eyes and stuffed his things into his saddlebags. Luckily for him, he'd packed those bags enough times that he could have done it in his sleep. This time wasn't too far from it. As he went through those motions, Clint considered slamming his door and getting some more sleep while Jake handled his own damn problems. The plain truth, however, was that he figured the fastest way to be rid of Jake was just to do this one favor as quickly as possible.

Besides, he did intend on leaving town that morning, so it was only a matter of a few hours' difference.

"I think those cowboys were getting their horses already," Jake said nervously. "That's why I came by to make sure you were up and ready."

"One out of two isn't bad," Clint muttered.

"What?"

"Never mind. I'm ready. Let's go."

Although Clint didn't look his Sunday best, he was covered and presentable when he left his room. His saddlebags were over his shoulder and his Colt was around his waist. By the time he was walking up to the front desk, most of the fog had even cleared from his eyes.

"I settled up your bill," Jake said while practically shoving Clint toward the front door.

"Really?"

To answer that question, the fellow behind the desk waved and nodded.

"Thanks," Clint said.

"The least I could do. I was going to bring your horse over as well, but he wouldn't have any of it. That's quite an animal."

Clint grinned at the thought of skinny Jake trying to grab Eclipse's reins and drag the stallion anywhere he didn't feel like going. "Why don't you get going?" Clint said. "I'll catch up."

Jake shook his head. "I'd rather not. Otherwise, I might as well go alone."

"Then how about filling a canteen with some coffee," Clint suggested. "Then we can have our little parade out of here."

Jake liked the sound of that and dashed back into the hotel's restaurant. When he came out again with the coffee, Clint was already riding Eclipse toward the front of the hotel. After tossing Clint the canteen, Jake hopped into his own saddle and snapped his reins.

While the skinny fellow might have seemed twitchy and awkward on his feet or anywhere else, Jake was a natural rider. He moved perfectly with the movements of his horse and knew just when to flick the reins and when to sit back and let the animal take over.

Eclipse caught up with Jake's horse before too long, which was a lot longer than it took for the Darley Arabian to catch up with most others. They flew away from town like it was on fire, thundering toward the state line as the sky started to smear with color behind them.

The further he rode, the more alive Clint felt. It was easy to stay bleary-eyed and sleepy in a hotel room, but it was impossible to stay that way when sitting on top of a lightning bolt. Eclipse's strides were so powerful that it felt like Clint was trying to sit on top of a steam engine. With the wind blasting his face and the ground rushing beneath him, Clint couldn't help but feel anxious to take on the world.

Apparently, he wasn't the only one to feel that way on that particular morning.

The cowboys announced themselves with a few hoots and hollers. They screamed at Clint and Jake while closing in on them from both sides. The sound of their horses could be heard even over the thunder of Eclipse's hooves mingling with that of Jake's horse.

Clint took a quick glance over both shoulders. That was all he needed to count two riders closing in from each side.

"That's more than I thought there would be," Jake shouted.

"Yeah," Clint replied. "I figured as much."

Clint had to laugh when he thought back to just before he'd left his hotel room. That was when he'd been convinced that helping Jake out now would be the quickest way to be rid of him and his troubles.

Now, it looked like Clint had a long way to go before getting any more peace and quiet.

EIGHT

The first few shots cracked through the air, spitting lead over Clint and Jake's heads.

"They're shooting at us!" Jake screamed.

"Really?" Clint asked as he drew the Colt from its holster. "I hadn't noticed." Before Jake could reply to that, Clint pointed the Colt toward the cowboys on his right and fired off a shot. It wasn't aimed at any of the cowboys in particular, but it did a great job of showing them he meant business.

"Don't you have a gun?" Clint asked.

Jake looked confused at first, but then he started to nod.

"At least skin the damn thing!"

Only after hearing that come from Clint's mouth did Jake reach for his pistol. It was an old .38 and looked as if it would just as soon blow up in Jake's hand as fire a shot at any of the cowboys.

"I never killed a man before!" Jake hollered as if he suddenly thought he was sitting in a confessional.

"I didn't ask you to kill anyone," Clint said. "Just shoot at them!"

Clenching his eyes shut and pointing his gun hand at the closest pair of cowboys, Jake gritted his teeth and pulled his trigger. The .38 didn't blow his hand off, but it did cause the two cowboys to scatter like a bunch of dry leaves.

Clint half expected to see one of those cowboys fall dead from his saddle. More trouble was caused when a shot was taken half-assed than when there was some thought behind it. This time, Jake's luck held and he didn't break his streak of not killing anyone.

The cowboys, on the other hand, didn't seem so concerned about such matters.

"Toss that money," one of the cowboys shouted between shots. "and maybe we'll let you run away!"

Clint focused on the one who was doing the talking, aimed his modified Colt, and fired off a shot. Even though both he and his target were moving, he knew he'd found his mark the moment he pulled his trigger. Sure enough, he saw the cowboy's hat fly off and his head snap back as if his neck had been snagged on a low-hanging branch.

A second later, the cowboy straightened up and patted the empty spot on top of his head where his hat had once been. There wasn't a drop of blood spilled, even though he could still feel the hot lead that had buzzed over his head like a hornet. Even after the other riders saw their partner was all right, they were slow to charge right after Jake and Clint. Instead, they separated in four different directions while falling back from the men they'd been chasing.

"See?" Jake shouted while hunkering down over his horse's back. "I told you they'd be after me!"

"What did you do to those boys to rile them up like this?" Clint asked.

"Nothing! They're after my money."

"They already won most of it."

"Yeah, but . . ." Jake trailed off as he pretended to fuss with the reins that were wrapped around his hand.

"But what?" Clint asked. "Tell me now or deal with these fellas yourself."

After shooting a few anxious glances over his shoulder,

Jake replied, "I may have gotten into another game with one of them."

"Jesus. Do you owe more money?"

"No, I paid up. I learned my lesson real good after the last time." Just as Jake said that, one of the cowboys fired a shot that whipped right between Clint's and Jake's heads. It seemed as though one of the cowboys didn't like what he'd heard or some higher power was putting Jake back in his place.

"I won a little more from them than they wanted," Jake continued.

"You cheated?"

"No, no! They just didn't like the way I . . . uh . . . celebrated my winning streak."

Like another punctuation from on high, two more shots cracked through the air. The cowboys were getting their courage back and had regrouped to close in on Clint and Jake from behind.

"You rubbed their noses in it," Clint stated. Imagining Jake doing such a thing was so easy for Clint that he didn't even need to hear him affirm the statement. Jake did glance over to him for a second, however, which was enough for Clint to see Jake's quick shrug and nod.

Although such a thing wasn't a shooting offense at a card table, it was something that anyone with common sense knew to avoid. And after being threatened by another player, even a dim-witted house cat would know better than to push his luck twice.

Despite all of that, Jake still didn't deserve to be killed for what he'd done.

Smacked around a bit, maybe, but not killed.

"Hand over the package," Clint said.

"What?"

"Hand it over. Quick!" As he said that, Clint steered Eclipse almost close enough to bump into the side of Jake's horse. He saw the bundle in Jake's hand and started to snatch it away from him. At the last second, he let go and left it in Jake's hand.

Clint lowered his voice so it could just be heard over the rumble of hooves and occasional gunshot. "They don't know who's got what now. On my signal, split off and ride as fast as you can until you lose whoever follows you. Circle around, make your delivery, and move on."

Jake nodded.

"Oh, and stay away from the card tables," Clint added. With that, he tucked his arm in close to his body, as if he had the package, and broke away. "NOW!" he shouted.

At that signal, Jake made a sharp turn in one direction while Clint turned in the other. For a second or two, the cowboys didn't know which one to follow. By the time they decided who would go with whom, Clint and Jake had built themselves a good lead.

When Clint glanced over his shoulder, there were only two men trying to catch up to him. He figured he'd keep riding until those two were lost in the dust. He expected them to keep up for a mile or two. They hung in for quite a bit more . . .

NINE

Clint didn't know what the hell Jake had done to these cowboys, but it must have been something big for them to keep after him for this long. He hadn't seen Jake since they'd split up, which had been over a day ago. In that time, Eclipse had been tearing up the ground beneath his hooves like a brushfire and seemed to be enjoying every last minute of it.

At first, Clint hadn't wanted to kill any of the cowboys if he could help it. But since they were doing their level best to put him down any time they were in firing range, Clint decided to pull out some of the stops himself. More of the cowboys had started to appear, which was most definitely not a good sign. Before he did anything else, Clint decided it was time to get a better handle on the situation.

Heading into Hendricks was a necessary part of the ruse. Otherwise, the cowboys wouldn't have followed him this far. Every so often, Clint would wonder why he was going through so much trouble to help a pain in the ass like Jake. He never really did come up with a good answer for that. Fortunately for Jake, the cowboys had become even bigger pains in the ass.

The rocks dipped and grew as Clint passed them. Formations flew by as larger ones drew closer. Every so often, Clint could see what had to be the town of Hendricks, but that wasn't what caught his interest. What Clint was after was a particular kind of rock formation. Fortunately, with so many nearby, he didn't have to wait too long before finding one that suited his purpose.

After pulling back on the reins a bit, Clint made his move and then gave Eclipse a slap on the rump to get the stallion moving again.

"Did you see that?" one of the cowboys said to the man riding next to him.

The second one squinted and shook his head. "All I see is a mess of dust. This shit's been getting in my eyes for too damn long."

"Well, I think I saw something. Head around that way in case that bastard makes another move. I'm heading this way."

"What did you see?"

"Never you mind! Just do what I say and make sure that stretch of trail is cut off!"

"Fine!"

The rocks had stretched out to cut the trail in two the way a fallen boulder might part a stream. The second cowboy turned to ride around one side of the rock while the first snapped his reins and got his horse bolting toward the dust Eclipse had kicked up moments ago.

When he got closer to one wall of rock that was slightly higher than his own head, the cowboy slowed down and squinted at the ground. "Come on out," he said with a sly grin. "I saw you drop from your horse. If you come out now, I'll take that package and be on my way."

The cowboy kept moving slowly down the trail. He looked ahead and saw Eclipse. That sight only made his smile grow even wider. "I see there ain't nobody on your horse," he said. "Come out and I'll let you live. You may even be able to crawl into town to see a doc—"

Before he could finish, the cowboy heard a scraping over his head and felt something heavy drop across the back of his shoulders. Before he knew what was happening, he was sliding from his saddle and twisting around to look up at the sky.

There was a sharp pain in the cowboy's legs, followed by another impact that drove all the air from his lungs.

For a few seconds, the cowboy couldn't breathe.

He could barely even focus his eyes.

Then, after a few quick blinks, he cleared his vision enough to make some sense out of what had just happened.

He was hanging upside down and someone was walking straight for him. He had to get to his gun before it was too late.

It was already too late.

Clint's face drew closer until it was all the cowboy could see. He reached out for something with one hand while grinning down at the cowboy the way a cat grinned at a mouse it had trapped under its paw.

"All right," Clint said. "Let's have us a little chat."

TEN

Clint used his left hand to pat the horse's side to calm the animal down. It took some doing, but that was understandable. After all, the horse did have a grown man hanging off of one of its sides.

The cowboy's foot had become tangled in his stirrup during the fall. Now, he hung by one leg and swung back and forth like a poorly made pendulum. When he tried to make a clumsy grab for one of the guns that hadn't been dropped already, the cowboy's hand was slapped away with ease.

"That's not a polite way to chat," Clint said after he'd disarmed the cowboy. "All I want is to ask a few questions."

The cowboy had an insult and a mouthful of spit ready to go, but he thought twice when he saw the seriousness on Clint's face.

Nodding, Clint said, "Where's Jake?"

"H—hell if I know. We lost him a long ways back."

"So you all came after me?"

"We knew you both was headed to Hendricks, so we just took the way we knew to get there."

Clint wasn't too surprised to hear that. It was just the way his luck had been running that the cowboys would simply catch up to him before they got to Jake. "What are you men after that dragged you all out here, anyway?"

"Don't you even know what you're carrying?"

Clint shook his head. "It's not my business to look into every package I see."

"That skinny little prick was carrying enough money to set up our whole crew for a few years. You know that damn well, since you saw just like I did what Jake was hiding under his saddle."

"Most of that was handed over already."

"Not according to your friend. He said he had more than enough left in that package to pay his way into the game being held in Hendricks."

"Game?"

The cowboy nodded. Since he was still upside down, that gesture made him a little green around the edges. "There's a big game coming up and it's invitation only. After beating us, thanks to the horseshoe stuck up his ass, Jake said he'd clean out that game, too."

"All of this is just about another card game?" Clint asked.

"We could win the rest of that money Jake's carrying. That'd fill all of our pockets! You could get in on it, too, if you wanted."

As Clint looked down at the cowboy, he shook his head and let out a measured breath. "You know something?"

"What?" the cowboy asked with a glimmer of hope in his eyes.

"I just realized why I went through so much trouble to help out Jake in the first place." Clint leaned in closer and added, "You and your friends are nothing but a bunch of cowardly back-shooters with bad tempers and greedy hearts. Your kind turn my stomach."

This time, the cowboy didn't hold back what he'd been saving at the back of his throat. "Fuck you!" When he tried to spit in Clint's face, he found himself dropping the rest of the way to the ground and landing with a jarring thump.

Clint kept shaking his head at the sight of the cowboy
spitting on himself as his shoulders and head knocked
against the ground. Drool mixed with a bit of blood
dripped down the cowboy's forehead and soaked into his
hair from the newly formed puddle on the ground.

"Men like you are so predictable," Clint mused. "It's no
wonder you can't come up with a way to make your own
damn money."

Struggling to right himself, the cowboy flopped in the
dirt like a fish out of water. "We'll have plenty of money
when we take it from you and that friend of yours! We'll all
be rich and we'll piss on both of your graves!"

As he finished his tirade, the cowboy yanked his foot
from the stirrup and scrambled to grab one of the guns he'd
dropped. Swinging the weapon up, he let out a single vic-
torious laugh, which bounced off the rocks.

There was nothing to aim at.

Clint was gone.

"Dammit!"

The rock that Clint had found and climbed was also big
enough for him to duck behind with just a few steps. He
could still hear the fallen cowboy kicking and screaming as
he dashed through a narrow gap between two rocks. Clint
didn't know where he would end up, but he could see the
other side of the narrow passage and that was good enough.

The rest of the cowboys were still about. Clint could
hear them shouting to each other from some other spot in
the pass. As soon as he emerged from the rocks, Clint let
out a sharp whistle. He didn't like the thought of giving
away his position, but it was a necessary evil.

Eclipse heard the whistle and came running. Clint spotted the Darley Arabian in a matter of seconds and stepped
out a little more so he could be seen. The stallion headed
straight for him, catching the attention of more than one of
the other cowboys.

That didn't matter to Clint. He'd seen enough of the pass as well as the cowboys themselves to know he could either lose them in the rocks or outrun them, thanks to Eclipse's raw power. All he needed was to get back in the saddle and pull off a few simple tricks to put those cowboys behind him for good.

Eclipse came straight to him and began to slow as he got closer. When Clint saw the Darley Arabian approach, he stepped out and began reaching up to take hold of the saddle horn and swing himself up. Since he was already thinking a few steps ahead, he didn't even feel the bite of steel puncturing his side right away.

It felt like a pinched muscle or even a bad cramp.

When the pain hit, it washed over him with a sickening wave that was something like being drunk.

"Got you, asshole," hissed another cowboy from directly behind Clint.

ELEVEN

Clint acted on nothing but instinct.

Balling up his fist, Clint raised his arm and snapped it back as if he was trying to pull down a barn with one hand. His elbow found its target and impacted with every bit of strength that its owner could muster. Clint felt something crunch against his elbow, but wasn't able to feel satisfied about it. He was in too much pain for that.

Eclipse rode right up to Clint, allowing him to reach up and grab hold of the saddle horn just as he'd planned. Clint hadn't been planning on getting stabbed in the process, though, and was lucky to hold on long enough to pull himself into the saddle.

Clint knew he'd been stabbed almost immediately after feeling that pinch. It wasn't the first time it had happened, but that didn't mean that he'd been looking forward to it. He knew all too well that any injury could be a man's last. Even walking across a street carried its own set of risks. Unfortunately, Clint's life was a hell of a lot riskier than most.

The blood flowed out of his back in a rush, soaking his shirt and sticking to his skin.

Clint was starting to get numb and he knew well enough that that wasn't a good thing.

"I got him!" the man with the knife shouted. "I stuck him good!"

The man with the bloody blade in his hand was the partner of the cowboy who had been dangling from his own stirrup a few moments ago. He was a big fellow with a wide face and dull eyes. His feet thumped against the dirt as he rushed toward Eclipse.

Clint wobbled a bit in the saddle, but settled in without too much trouble, since riding Eclipse was akin to walking a straight line. When he felt a hand grab hold of his ankle, Clint looked down at the fat face of the man who'd stabbed him.

The man with the knife had a face full of blood, thanks to the broken nose Clint's elbow had given him. Even with his nose cocked at an odd angle and blood pouring over his face, the fat man grabbed hold of Clint as if he'd caught the prize goose at a county fair.

Eclipse was raring to go, but held back when he felt that something was still tying him to his spot.

Clint's first instinct was just to push the fat man away. He tried kicking at him, but the man's grip was too tight and his fist was so meaty that it enveloped his ankle completely. Clint then tried to swing a fist down at the man's face, but it bounced off the bloodied flesh like a wet noodle.

"You got him?" the cowboy on the other side of the rocks shouted. "Hold him there! I'll make him pay for knocking me around like that!"

The fat man grinned and nodded, even though his partner wasn't in sight.

Clint knew he didn't have much time before the rest of those cowboys swarmed all over him to tear him apart. Gathering up what was left of his strength, Clint sent another punch toward the fat man's face. This time, he aimed for the broken mess that had been the guy's nose.

Somehow, the fat man managed to catch Clint's fist just before it hit its target.

Clint was stunned by the move.

The fat man merely shook his head and glared up into Clint's eyes. "Maybe I won't wait for the others," he said in a slow drawl. With that, he raised his other hand, which was still wrapped around the knife.

That blade sliced through the air, making a line directly for Clint's throat.

Clint sat in his saddle and watched it come at him as if he was watching a performance on a stage. His senses were blurring and his strength drained from him along with the blood seeping from his wound. The blade seemed to be taking a long time in getting to him, but he had no doubt it would get there all the same.

Suddenly, a shot blasted through the air and snapped Clint out of his daze.

His body was still going numb, so he didn't feel much pain.

After a second had dragged by, Clint felt that his left arm was extended and weighed down. Another blink was enough for him to see he was holding his Colt in an awkward left-handed grip. Smoke was curling from the barrel.

The fat man still looked at Clint with a blank stare. His grip around Clint's fist loosened and he staggered back. The blood on his face was thicker than a mask. It was so thick it nearly covered the fresh hole that had been blasted through his cheek.

Clint shoved the fat man back and snapped his reins. Although he was surprised he'd drawn and fired the Colt with his left hand, he wasn't surprised he'd hit his target. The fat man was so close it would have taken more effort to miss him.

As soon as he felt the leather snap, Eclipse was off and running. The Darley Arabian's muscles twitched and the blood surged through his veins after all those shots had been fired and blood had been spilled. Since there was only one way to steer between those rocks, Eclipse took off in that direction without needing any more help from Clint.

That was good for Clint, since he wasn't in the condition to do much more than struggle to keep his balance in the saddle. His body shifted reflexively to match Eclipse's movements and his limbs went through their own motions that were easier than second nature.

Behind him, Clint could hear the excited voices of the cowboys echoing between the rocks. Those voices mixed with the sounds of hooves clattering against the stony ground until no single source for the noise could be distinguished from the whole.

Clint tapped his heels against Eclipse's sides and hung on as tightly as he could. The Darley Arabian put even more power into his stride until he was charging at a strong gallop. Clint couldn't see exactly where he was going.

His eyes were drooping and he was fighting to stay conscious.

Being jostled in the saddle wasn't helping his knife wound, but there wasn't much to be done about that.

Eclipse had just saved his life and Clint figured he'd count his blessings and try to survive the next few minutes.

TWELVE

The Learner place was a spread situated close enough to
Hendricks to make it an easy ride into town, but far enough
away for the family not to be bothered by the noises coming from the more-populated area. It was a small farm that
raised what few animals Old Man Learner could afford.
That meant there were a few pens and a small barn to com-
pliment the house, which the Learners had built with their
own hands.

Amelia Learner rounded the corner and immediately
saw that the fences of one of the largest pigpens was shat-
tered and busted wide open. She might have noticed that
the pigs were out and exploring the nearby land if a large
stallion wasn't standing in the middle of the wet mud.

"Oh, my lord!" Amelia shouted as she dropped the
buckets she'd been carrying and held her hands up to her
face.

Before she could call for him, Amelia's father raced
around the other side of the barn with a long hunting rifle
gripped in his hands. "Step back, sweetie," he said. "I saw
what happened."

Amelia was in her mid-twenties, with a slender build.
She wore a light-blue dress with an apron tied around her

46

waist in preparation for her daily chores. Her long, dark
hair was tied back and her brown eyes were wide with surprise of what she saw.

"What happened?" she asked.

"That man there rode his horse into our pigpen. That's
what happened. He's probably a drunk from one of the saloons in town."

Leaning forward and narrowing her eyes, Amelia said,
"Looks like he's hurt."

"He fell off his horse. Don't worry. Drunks usually walk
away from a fall just fine."

"He's bleeding."

Frank Learner stepped forward and moved his daughter
aside. "Just step back and let me handle this. I don't want
some dirty drunk taking hold of you."

Amelia stepped back and let her father walk toward the
pen. Since Frank was more concerned with the man lying
in the mud, he didn't seem to notice the way the horse eyed
him as he drew closer to the broken fence. Knowing that
her father would only push her back again, Amelia walked
toward the horse and held out her hand.

Eclipse's muscles were tense as he stood between Clint
and Frank. He was less accustomed to Clint falling from
the saddle than he was to all the gunfire. Sensing that Clint
was hurt only made the stallion that much more nervous.

"It's all right, boy," she whispered while extending her
hand. "Nobody's gonna hurt you or anyone else." She
paused when Eclipse gave her a strong snort.

Even Frank came to a halt when he felt Eclipse's hoof
stomp against the ground. "Maybe I should deal with this
horse first," he said.

"I'll do that," Amelia said. Without waiting for a response, she stepped a little closer to Eclipse and then
reached out for the reins.

The Darley Arabian pulled his head back and shook it,
but that didn't stop Amelia. Although she pulled her hand

back, she reached right out again and even managed to grab Eclipse's bridle.

"There, now," she whispered soothingly. "I said I wasn't going to hurt you. Now just come along out of that mud."

Although Eclipse wasn't willing to leave Clint lying there, he did calm down enough to let Frank get a little closer. Amelia coaxed the stallion out a little further, but Eclipse wasn't about to let Clint out of his sight.

Frank stood his ground a few feet away from Clint. He seemed to be satisfied with standing in that spot and glaring down at Clint over the barrel of his hunting rifle. "You there! What the hell are you doing on my property?"

Clint stirred and shifted on the ground. He let out a confused groan as he tried to get up, but only made it a few inches from the mud before falling back down again.

"He's hurt," Amelia said. "Can't you see that?"

"Drunks get hurt all the time," Frank grumbled. "Usually, they got it coming to them."

"I'm not . . . drunk," Clint said.

"Yeah? Then how do you explain riding your horse straight into my pigs?"

"I must've blacked out." Talking was forcing Clint to focus more on his surroundings. Although his vision was slowly coming into place, he didn't feel anxious to make another go of getting to his feet. The pain from his wound was returning like a burn from a branding iron in his back.

"What happened to you?" Amelia asked.

"Got stabbed."

"You see?" Amelia said to her father. "He's hurt. Now can we please just bring him inside before he dies in that mud?"

Frank held his ground for another few seconds before slowly lowering his gun. "I suppose he does look cut up. It wouldn't look good to have a man die out here in one of my pens."

"That's the spirit." Amelia sighed. "Now are you going

to help me carry him inside, or would you rather point that gun at the both of us while I do all the work?"

Frank gnashed his teeth together while his daughter pushed by him. "He's not some stray dog, damn it. Don't you see that gun he's wearing?"

"I also see that your gun is plenty bigger than his, so just keep a hold of that while I do this."

"Do what? Amelia! Don't!"

But none of Frank's words landed. Amelia had already stepped into the pen and stooped down to get a closer look at Clint. After a few whispered words between them, she slid her arm around him and helped him to his feet.

Frank looked on, not liking what he saw. He knew his daughter well enough, however, to know that there wasn't much he could do to stop her at this point. Instead, Frank kept his rifle pointed at Clint while Amelia helped drag him to the house.

THIRTEEN

"He is bleeding a hell of a lot," Frank grumbled as Clint was lowered onto a bed in the Learners' home.

Amelia had yet to take her eyes off of Clint and was busy trying to make sure he wasn't going to roll off the bed. "That's what I said from the start. Now are you going to put that gun down or would you like to stand guard over him while he's passed out?"

"He ain't passed out," Frank said, while still glaring at Clint over the barrel of the hunting rifle. When Frank saw Clint's arm move, he tightened his finger a bit more around his trigger and steadied his aim.

"Here," Clint said softly while taking hold of his Colt between his thumb and forefinger. "Might as well . . . hold on to it."

For a moment, Frank didn't seem to know what to do. After he saw the gun dangling harmlessly between Clint's fingers, he reached out to snatch it away. He still kept the rifle pointed at Clint until the Colt was completely out of its owner's grasp. Even then, Frank took a few steps back before lowering the rifle.

"Dave!" Frank shouted.

The older man's voice echoed inside the small room. That sound was soon followed by the approach of quick footsteps. A young man who looked to be in his mid-teens shoved his way into the room and took in the sights with wide eyes. Between the bloody stranger laying on the bed and all the guns in view, he couldn't decide what to look at next.

"What is it, Pa?" Dave asked.

"Take this," Frank said as he handed Clint's pistol over to the boy.

"Wow! Is that man a gunfighter?"

"Never you mind about that. Just take it and hide it."

"Hide it where?"

"The same place you hid that cigar I told you not to smoke."

Dave averted his eyes for a moment and winced. "Yes, sir." The moment he got his hands on the modified Colt, however, the excited gleam snapped back into his eyes. That gleam faded just a bit when he wasn't able to wrangle the gun free from Frank's grasp.

Pulling the Colt away, Frank set his rifle against the wall so he could empty the bullets from the Colt. Only after the gun was empty did he hand it over to his son. "Now you won't blow your damn foot off by mistake."

Although he was clearly disappointed to handle the unloaded gun, Dave was still mighty happy to finally get the Colt to himself. Holding it in his best depiction of a gunfighter's grip, he marched out of the room and to his hiding place.

When Frank turned his eyes back to the bed, he was still suspicious. He wasn't, however, looking over the barrel of his rifle. "Who are you, mister?"

"Name's . . . Clint Adams."

"What are you doing on my property?"

"Mistake. I must have . . ."

"He's hurt and his horse brought him here," Amelia said impatiently. "I can see that just as well as anyone else can. He needs a doctor, not a conversation."

"We'll see about that," Frank said. Rolling up his sleeves, he approached the bed and lowered himself down to get a look at Clint's wound. "Strip away them clothes."

Amelia carefully pulled Clint's shirt from where it was tucked into his pants. She winced when she saw Clint start to squirm in pain, but continued to do what her father had asked. After a few more careful movements, she had Clint's shirt rolled up high enough for the knife wound to be fully exposed.

"It doesn't look so bad," she said.

Frank shook his head. "It don't need to look bad on the outside. It's what's inside that matters. Fetch me some water and your needle and thread."

"Or I could just fetch a doctor from town."

"Look at him, Amelia," Frank said while motioning toward the bed. Clint's face looked pale and waxy. His eyes were starting to glaze over. "He's lucky he made it this far. The last thing he needs is to wait any longer for someone to do something."

"And I suppose you know what to do?"

"I got you back in proper order when you broke your arm and leg while you were a kid. I saw to your brother when he fell on that fence post, didn't I?"

Amelia nodded.

"I know what needs to be done," Frank continued. "It's not that hard. He'll be doing the hard part by just trying to sit still long enough for me to finish the job. Now go get those things I asked for and be quick about it. I'll need your help in this, too, you know."

Amelia got to her feet and rushed to collect the items Frank had requested. Before too long, she was back with a full washbasin in both hands and a few rags over her shoulder. After setting the basin down, she sat on the edge of the bed and fished a needle and thread from her pocket.

"That the thickest thread you got?" Frank asked.

"It is."

"Good, then I suppose you know what you're going to have to do. I'll clean off the wound and you thread that needle."

"But, I don't think I can—"

"You'll have to," Frank interrupted. "I can't sew half as good as you. My hands ain't steady like that no more. Don't worry about it. I'll help you through it."

Trying to calm her nerves, Amelia prepared a few needles while Frank wet down some of the rags and washed up the wound. Most of the blood had scabbed over, but all the shifting upon the bed had reopened the gash and the blood was flowing once more.

"You ready?" Frank asked. "He's bleeding again."

"Ready as I'll ever be," she replied.

"Good. Now just sew him up like you'd sew up a ripped tablecloth."

She reached out toward Clint's wound, but stopped and pulled her arms back. "I can't."

"Yes you can," Frank said sternly. "You wanted to help him, so this is what we've got to do. Now do it or get him out of my house."

Amelia pulled in a deep breath, steeled herself, and started to sew.

FOURTEEN

There was a while when Clint couldn't decide if he was asleep, awake, or somewhere in between. His vision would fade in and out amid jabs of pain that were just strong enough for him to feel like a small animal was nipping at his side.

When he did manage to see through the fog that filled his skull, he saw the inside of a room. Eventually, a dim light flickered upon the walls and rafters over his head. Still, he couldn't quite tell whether or not he was actually in that room or merely imagining it.

His head was spinning.

Clint thought back to the cowboys who had tried to ambush him and swore he'd gotten away from them.

Then again, if he thought about it for long enough, he could recall things ending in a much different way.

Finally, Clint decided not to think about it at all for a while. If he was dreaming, he might as well let it play itself out. If he was awake, he wasn't in good enough shape to do himself any good for the moment. If he was dead, he'd still be dead after he took a few moments to relax and pull himself together.

All Clint had to do was stop struggling and all the rest

just faded away. He dropped into a comfortable blackness that wrapped around him like sheets that had been cooled in front of an open window. The pain receded.

Soon, there was nothing but quiet.

Suddenly, pain stabbed through Clint's side. It was enough to snap him out of his quiet calm and force him to open his eyes. The lids were stuck against his cheek and came open like dirty paper being peeled off a wall. When he tried to sit up, he only made it halfway before being stopped by something directly in front of him.

". . . try and move," came a voice from off to Clint's side.

Trying to turn and look at who'd spoken only made the pain in his side worse. Feeling that forced the world into sharp focus and gave Clint a real quick answer to one of the questions floating through his mind.

He most definitely wasn't dead.

A woman's face, framed by dark hair, filled Clint's vision. Brown eyes soft with concern were focused upon him. She was reaching out with both hands to gently push Clint back down onto the bed. "I said you shouldn't try to move. You might rip those stitches again."

Clint let out a breath and allowed himself to be pushed down. His head fell onto a fluffy pillow and his back was supported by a firm mattress. After feeling that, he wasn't so anxious to get up again.

"Do you remember how you got here?" she asked.

Closing his eyes, Clint sifted through the memories. Like gold dust glittering through the silt, the real memories quickly separated themselves from the dreams. "Yeah," Clint rasped. "I remember something about a . . . a bunch of pigs."

The woman's face broke into a smile as she leaned back into her chair and nodded. "That's right. I found you laying in our pigpen."

"Normally . . ." Clint croaked, before clearing his throat and trying again. "Normally, I prefer the front door."

She laughed and turned in her chair. When she turned back to face Clint again, she was holding a tin cup in her hands. "Here. Drink some water. It'll make your throat feel better."

Clint pushed himself up so he was sitting with his back supported against the headboard. He took the cup he was offered and drank some water. It splashed against the back of his throat, hurting at first, but still feeling awfully good. The second sip went down without a hitch. "Thanks."

"Would you like some more?"

"Yes, please."

She left the room, allowing Clint to take a look around for himself. Now that he'd thought it over for a bit, he did recognize the place. At least, he recognized it as the same place where he'd fallen asleep.

Amelia returned with the cup of water. She was wearing a dark green dress with thin, white stripes. She walked with her head tilted down, but she had nothing at all to be ashamed about. Her trim figure was rounded in all the right places and her hips moved nicely under her skirt. When she noticed that Clint was studying her, she blushed a bit and smirked before sitting on the chair next to the bed.

"I didn't catch your name," Clint said as he took the water.

"It's Amelia Learner."

"I'm Clint Adams." Lifting the cup in a toast, he added, "Pleased to make your acquaintance."

She nodded somewhat formally and folded her hands upon her lap.

As Clint sipped from the cup, he felt the twinge of pain in his side. Reaching down with one hand, he inspected the wound and ran his fingertips over the rows of thread holding him together. "Do I have you to thank for the stitches?"

She nodded. "All five sets of them."

"Five sets?"

"I've never done stitches before. Well . . . not on a person, anyway. It took me two times to get them right. You tore another two sets out while you tossed in your sleep."

Clint thought back to his dreams and tried to trace them back to when he'd fallen asleep. It didn't seem like more than an hour or two since the nipping at his side had stopped. "How long was I out?" he asked.

"Three days."

"Three days?"

She nodded. "You didn't wake up once. Not even when we had to take you out of those clothes you were wearing when you got here."

Looking down at himself, Clint jumped a bit in surprise when he saw the loose old shirt that was practically hanging off his shoulders. The buttons were misaligned and the bottom portion was twisted around his torso.

"It's my father's," Amelia explained. "Your clothes are soaking. Hopefully, most of the blood and dirt will come out."

Clint lifted the sheet a bit more and saw that he was wearing a faded set of long johns that he hadn't been wearing before. "I hope these don't belong to your father as well."

"They were going to. I was saving them for his birthday, but you needed them more."

"I really appreciate all of this," Clint said as he let the sheet fall back into place. "I just hope I haven't been too much trouble."

Amelia shook her head. "It's no trouble. I'm just glad you're going to make it through alive. You looked so bad when I found you. I thought you might not pull through."

"I'll be fine," Clint said as he carefully felt around the edges of his wound. "My jacket must have kept the blade from going in too deep."

"That's what my father said."

"Well, your father's a smart fellow. I'd like to thank him as well, if he's about."

"He'll come by soon enough." The way Amelia said that, it was clear she wasn't too eager for that to happen.

"If he'd prefer, I could get on my way," Clint offered.

"No, no. You stay put. He's just worried that you might die on his land or that some other men might come after you."

"While we're on that subject," Clint said, "there's something else I need to ask. Were there any men that came around looking for me?"

Amelia shook her head without hesitation. "No," she said with a warm smile. "You're the only one that's been here. Stay as long as you need."

FIFTEEN

Clint had a hard time believing that he'd been out of sorts for three days. That became a little easier to swallow when he swung his feet over the side of the bed and tried to get up. His legs barely had any feeling in them at all and when the blood did start to flow, it was more uncomfortable than the stitches in his back.

"Here," Amelia said as she reached out to take his arm. "Let me help you."

"Just give me a moment," Clint said.

She stood back, but didn't go far.

After a minute or so had passed, the prickling sensation in Clint's legs began to recede and he tried to get up again. Although he had an easier time of it, he still accepted Amelia's help before he was able to support his weight on his own.

"There you go," she said. "Good as new."

"I don't know about that, but it feels pretty close."

They made it to the door before being stopped by another of the Learners.

"He ain't supposed to come out of there," came the stern voice of the room's self-appointed guard.

Amelia nearly backhanded her brother as she said, "Step aside, Dave, and get ready for supper."

Although he didn't have any choice but to move, Dave fixed a glare upon Clint that was meant to be threatening. It came off like a puppy trying to stare down a hungry wolf.

"All right," Dave said. "But I'm telling Pa about you bringing him out of that room."

"Good. While you're at it, be sure to tell him supper's ready."

"Yeah, yeah," Dave grumbled. The boy headed for the front door and walked outside, clearing the way for Clint to see most of the rest of the house.

The dining room was straight ahead and a modest table was set for four. Smells drifted from the adjacent kitchen, tempting Clint's nose and making his stomach growl loudly. To the right, there was a sitting room and fireplace. It wasn't a fancy home by any stretch, but it was warm and very comfortable.

"Is that chicken I smell?" Clint asked.

"It sure is. I hope you don't mind."

"Fried chicken?"

"Yes, sir."

"That smell just proves that something good can come out of anything. Even getting stabbed."

Amelia laughed and slowly let go of Clint's arm. When she saw he could walk just fine on his own, she headed for the kitchen. "There's also some potatoes, bread, and some corn. I figured you'd be hungry after all that time you spent sleeping."

"He better be hungry," Frank said as he stomped in through the front door. "Because Amelia's been cooking a feast every night since you got here."

Clint looked over and saw the older man studying him with cold, sharp eyes. He'd been just about to lower himself into a chair, but held off so he could extend a hand in

Frank's direction. "I'm obliged for everything you've done, sir. Thank you."

Frank nodded and reluctantly gave Clint's hand a shake. "Thank my daughter. She's the one that's been looking after you."

"Day and night, night and day," Dave said in a taunting voice.

"Shut up, Dave," Amelia said in a voice that made it clear who was the older sister and who was the younger brother.

Deferring to the natural pecking order between siblings, Dave lowered his head a bit and glared at her. He did, however, keep his mouth shut as ordered.

Frank settled into his seat at the head of the table and waited quietly for Amelia to start bringing out the food. When the plate was set down in front of him, he immediately picked up a fork and dug in.

"Since you're feeling good enough to talk," Frank said, "maybe you could tell us about what brought you to my pigpen."

"He's a Darley Arabian, sir," Clint said with a straight face.

For a moment, there was nothing but silence surrounding Clint's attempt at humor. Then, Dave finally understood the joke and broke out in laughter.

"Shut up, Dave," Frank said without taking his eyes from Clint. "What I wanted to know was how you wound up stabbed and dumped onto my property."

"I know what you meant," Clint said. "I was just trying to lighten the mood."

"My mood's just fine."

"All right, then." Just as he was about to start talking, Clint saw Amelia reappear and set a plate in front of him. The food smelled even better up close and Amelia accompanied it with a subtle roll of her eyes aimed in her father's direction.

"Perhaps my daughter thinks I'm a bit too forward with my questions," Frank said.

"It's understandable, sir," Clint replied. "I was riding with a courier across the state line and we were ambushed. We split up and some of the men that ambushed us caught up to me and started shooting again. Actually, to tell the truth, they were shooting at me from the moment I started out on that ride."

"Courier, huh? What was he carrying?"

"The men that attacked us were after the courier's money," Clint said after taking a bite of fried chicken. "There was some bad blood between them."

"I'd say there was. I'd also say it would be hard for you to get stabbed if all you did was ride across the state line while firing a gun."

"I had to get off my horse at one point. That's when I got stabbed."

Frank nodded as if he was listening to Judas himself try to defend his actions.

"Like I told your daughter, I don't want to impose," Clint explained. "This meal and everything else you've done for me is more than generous. If there's any way I can repay you, just say so. Otherwise, I'll be more than happy to move on and leave you folks in peace."

Pulling in a breath while gripping his fork, Frank was just about to say something when Amelia cut him off.

"You can stay as long as you like," she said. "I'm sure my father wouldn't want to let you leave until you were healed up properly." Turning her eyes toward the head of the table, she added, "Isn't that right, Pa?"

For a few moments, Frank's expression might as well have been chiseled out of solid rock. To be more precise, it could have been chiseled out of solid rock that had been frozen for about a hundred years at the darkest pit in the bottom of an ocean. In a few more seconds, however, the ice started to melt and he nodded. "He can stay." Frank looked Clint in the eyes and said, "You can stay. My apologies, but a man can't be too careful when he's looking after his family."

"That's perfectly understandable," Clint said. "I truly would like to know if there's anything I can do to repay your hospitality."

"Nonsense," Frank said. "Just eat your food and get the hell out of my house."

Everyone was silent until Frank let out a bark of a laugh.

"What?" the older man said. "Is he the only one that gets to make a joke round here?"

SIXTEEN

As night fell, the tall, flat rock formations looked like giants that had lain down and rolled over to go to sleep. Once the stars were fully visible overhead, the terrain was illuminated with a new set of lights. It was the same rocky pass that the cowboys had ridden through before, but now it looked pale and cold.

It looked dead. And the blood staining the dirt looked more like dried tar.

Only two figures were moving out there. Both of them were on horseback and neither of them was very happy.

"How the hell could we have lost him?" the first cowboy snarled.

"We shot him, stabbed him, ran him down. Hell, maybe he's tougher than we thought."

"He was stabbed. That's all we know for sure. Otherwise, he'd be laying right here in front of me."

The second cowboy chewed on the inside of his cheek while staring off at the distant town. "Well, I know he was stabbed. I saw the blood."

"Right. That means he's either dead somewhere or he's holed up and licking his wounds."

"Guess that's just as good as us killing him outright,"

the second cowboy said with a sigh. "You know, I hear Hendricks has some of the prettiest whores outside of California."

But the first man was already shaking his head. "We don't have time for that shit now. We've got us a wounded man to catch."

"Aw, for Christ's sake, Red! Didn't we already chase him far enough? For all we know, Jake's still got what we're after!"

"We'll know that for certain in a bit. Until then, we lay low and let our wounded friend get nice and comfortable until he feels good enough to stick his head out again. If he's got what we're after, we shouldn't have any trouble finishing him off."

"And what if Jake's still got it?"

"Then we go after him and finish off this asshole later. After he shot up one of my men, I ain't about to let him get healthy again."

The second man shifted in his saddle until enough time had passed for him to speak without being cut off. When he did talk again, he said, "Until them others come back with the news, why can't we go into town?"

Red looked at his partner and laughed. "You'd rather dip your wick than try to get rich?"

"Money comes and goes. A man don't get to see the prettiest whores this side of California every day."

Gazing at the town in the distance, Red contemplated that and smiled. "I like the way you think, Harry."

For the next few moments, both cowboys silently mulled over the joys awaiting them in Hendricks. The silence was broken by Harry's voice when he said, "I still don't see why we're so fired up to get these guys. I mean, we did chase them all the way into another state like they was dogs with their tails between their legs. Isn't that enough?"

"Enough? Not when you consider what it is that Jake was carrying."

"What's that?"

"Let's just say I got it on good authority that it's a hell of a lot more valuable than the cash stuffed under that asshole's saddle. The man that told me about it will make us rich if we get our hands on it."

"Rich?"

Red nodded and smiled even wider. "Every last one of us."

SEVENTEEN

"That," Clint said as he leaned back from the table and patted his stomach, "was one hell of a good meal."

Frank got up and said, "Judging by how much you ate, I was starting to think your stomach was cut open rather than getting that hole in your back."

"Guess a few days of sleep will do that to a man." Just hearing that caused Clint to wrinkle his brow and strain to think back through all that time. "Are you certain I was out that long?"

Amelia came from the kitchen to gather up the rest of the plates. "I am absolutely certain."

"And she should know," Frank replied. "Apart from changing you into them knickers you're wearing, she did all the work of looking after you."

"Like I said. If there's anything I can do—"

Before Clint could finish his offer, he was slapped on the shoulder as Frank walked by. "For right now, why don't you join me out on the porch?"

"Sounds good."

Clint stepped outside and was treated to a cool breeze the moment he walked through the door. That fresh air cleared him out like a broom sweeping out all the dust from an attic. When he pulled in a second lungful, he felt just a bit lightheaded.

"Bet it feels good to be outside, eh?" Frank asked.

"Like you wouldn't believe."

Digging into his pocket, Frank produced two cigars and handed one of them to Clint. "Let's just see if it can't get a little better."

Although Clint wasn't much for cigars, he didn't want to refuse the older man's hospitality. After all, it wasn't until just a few minutes ago that Frank stopped looking as if he wanted to gut Clint and hang him out to dry.

"Thanks," Clint said as he took the cigar. A few seconds later, Frank struck a match and used it to light them both.

The cigar tasted a bit like aged cedar, which was a little different than some of the others Clint had smoked. Even so, it wasn't entirely bad. Frank puffed on his own cigar and then let out a breath of smoke, which drifted up toward the stars.

"So, tell me, Clint. Are you a hired gun or a wanted man?"

The suddenness of the question almost caused the smoke to catch in the back of Clint's throat. "Pardon me?"

"Dave was right about that gun of yours. It looks like something carried by someone who makes his living with it. Since I didn't see a badge on you anywhere, that only leaves a few other possibilities."

"I guess I can see what you mean, but neither one of those two possibilities fits me very well."

"All right, then. Tell me what does fit you." The serious tone wasn't just back in Frank's voice, it was stronger than ever.

"My name is Clint Adams." When he said that, Clint watched Frank's face to see if those words hit any sort of chord. This was one of those rare occasions when the one who heard his name didn't seem to recognize it in the slightest. It was also one of the rare occasions when that wasn't a good thing.

"So you're a wanted man?"

"Not exactly, but my name is fairly well known to some folks."

"If it don't have anything to do with my family or my land, I don't pay much attention to it."

"I'm a gunsmith by trade. In fact, I put together that Colt myself."

"Impressive," Frank said with a nod. "You don't normally hear about gunsmiths using their own weapons so often."

"And that's why I'm somewhat well known. When I'm not working as a gunsmith, I travel and lend a hand where it's needed."

"By that, you mean you throw in on a fight when it suits you."

Shrugging, Clint said, "That's pretty close to the fact. I help when I can. Along the way, I've met up with plenty of lawmen that would vouch for me. As for wanted men, I've hauled in plenty of those as well."

"Is that what you were doing when you caught that blade in your back?"

"No, sir. I was doing just what I told you I was doing. A courier knew he was in for a hard ride and asked if I could come along to take some of the heat off of him. Things were pushed too far and I got hurt in the process."

"Where did this all start?" Frank asked.

"About ten miles or so across the state line."

Frank's cigar glowed in the night as he pulled in some more of the fragrant smoke. "That must have been one hell of an important courier for someone to chase him so far. Not to mention chasing and stabbing someone that was just riding alongside of him."

"Yeah," Clint said as those words began to sink in even deeper. "Seems that way, doesn't it?"

"You sound like this is the first time you thought this over."

"To be honest, it's the first time I've had a quiet moment to do any thinking about it. I was off and running, dodging bullets and fighting to survive almost the moment I started in on the job."

"Courier a friend of yours, then?"

"No," Clint said with a laugh. "He was actually such a pain in my ass that I wanted to do what I could to get him on his way so I wouldn't have to see or hear him anymore."

"Yeah," Frank said with the cigar clenched between his teeth. "I've had a few friends like that, myself. Them are the ones that seem to get you into the most trouble."

Clint's stitches pinched him just then, as if responding to the other man's words. "They sure do." But, more than the pain in his back or anywhere lower, Clint was concerned with the situation in general. He could see why a bunch of hotheaded cowboys would want to run someone like Jake out of town. Chasing Jake and Clint for as long as they did and with as much fire in their eyes as there was just didn't fit.

Something was missing from the picture and Clint knew that if he didn't find out what it was, that missing piece would become a bigger thorn in his side than Jake ever was.

EIGHTEEN

The wind blew between the broken boards like breath through cracked teeth. It whistled and shrieked, shaking the crooked wall against the nails that held it in place. If the old shack hadn't been shaken up so much already, there might have been dust coming down from the rafters. But the shack had managed to stay upright for several years, which was plenty long enough for all the dust to have been shaken loose already.

It was hard to tell what the shack's original purpose had been. It wasn't around any other shacks, so it couldn't have been part of an abandoned town. It was too well built for it to have been left over from an old camp and it was too small to have been a barn.

More than likely, the shack had been somebody's home a number of years ago. The bigger question was why anyone would want to live out in the middle of nowhere without anything but dry land for scenery and coyotes for neighbors.

Those things weren't a concern of the shack's current resident, however. Jake McKean huddled in there with his coat wrapped tightly around him to fend off the air that seemed to be getting colder and colder as the night wore on.

Jake's slender frame felt every lick of that wind until his blood ran cold just from the sound of it. He held his hands up to his mouth and breathed into his palms. That warmed him for a few seconds, as he stomped his feet and shoved his hands back into his pockets.

"Jesus Christ, this is a cold night," Jake muttered. "How you doing over there, Willie?"

At the opposite end of the room, Jake's horse stood in place and shifted from one hoof to another. The animal let out a huffing breath and shook its mane absently.

"You said it," Jake grunted. "This place is hell on earth. You think I should make a fire or would that draw too much attention?"

As before, the horse looked as though it barely even noticed that Jake was there.

"I suppose you're right. If we don't stay warm, we might be harming ourselves more than those cowboys ever could. A small fire shouldn't hurt."

Jake gathered up some garbage that was scattered throughout the shack and piled it beneath a few broken planks. The wind made it somewhat difficult, but he was able to get a fire started relatively easily. As soon as the flames started to crackle, Jake practically stuck his hands directly into them.

"Ah, now that's better! What do you think?"

Willie shifted from one spot to another while staring at a dark stain on the floor.

"I knew you'd like it!"

While squatting on the floor beside the fire, Jake rubbed his hands together and thought back about the last few days' events. He'd tried getting into Hendricks several times, but only got close enough to see the cowboys keeping watch and waiting for him to arrive. After circling the town more times than he could count, he'd decided to head back out and wait for things to cool off.

So far, the only thing cooling off was the air at night.

"Maybe we should try riding in a few hours before dawn," Jake muttered. "When it's so dark that nobody could see me until I was already past them. What do you think about that?"

Willie was drifting off to sleep.

"I wonder where Clint is. Maybe he already . . ."

Jake stopped short and snapped his head up like a rabbit that had just caught an unfamiliar scent. Huddling in place without moving a muscle, Jake was only distracted when his hand stayed a little too close to the flames.

For a moment, the only sound was the wind whistling through the wall.

Then, just beneath the surface of that wind, Jake could hear a metallic click.

He jumped to his feet just as the door of the shack was kicked in by a broad-shouldered man wearing a dark jacket. He was carrying a pistol in his hand, the same one that had been cocked only a few moments ago.

Jake's heel caught on one of the many imperfections in the floor. As he was stumbling over one of those boards, he managed to draw his gun and cock back the hammer. The weapon may have been an older model, but it was still reliable enough to fire when he pulled the trigger.

That first shot exploded inside the shack and drilled a hole in the wall a foot or two from the door frame. The kick of the gun wasn't too much, but it was enough to take away what remained of Jake's balance and send him falling backward to the floor.

Another shot blasted through the air. This one came from the cowboy who was stepping into the shack. His bullet might have caused Jake some pain if Jake had been standing in the spot where he'd previously been. Since Jake was currently falling on his ass, the bullet hissed over him and punched straight through another wall.

Jake gritted his teeth as pain shot up from his tailbone and lanced up into his stomach. It was pure survival instinct that got him to pull back the hammer and fire his gun once more. This time, he managed to hit his target.

The big cowboy standing in the doorway howled in agony as Jake's round shredded through his calf and splintered the bone in his leg. When he stumbled back to bounce off the wall, he wound up sliding down and coming to a rest upon the floor.

Behind the first cowboy, another man was standing with a shotgun in both hands. He looked stunned at seeing his partner drop, but quickly shifted his eyes to the man who'd dropped him.

"I got you now!" the second cowboy said. With that, he held up the shotgun and pulled one of its triggers.

The weapon let out a roar that deafened everyone in the shack. Smoke billowed outward and a storm of lead filled the air.

Jake curled up in a defensive ball and threw both arms over his head. He felt lead pellets rip through his shoulder and forearm, but the most pain came from one that nicked his elbow. The damage was inflicted upon his left side, allowing him to raise his pistol with his right arm and take another shot.

Even though the shot had been taken out of panic, it was close enough to make the shotgunner duck down low and wait before firing his second barrel.

Through the ringing in his ears, Jake was barely able to hear a sound that was much more familiar. Willie was bucking and whinnying behind him, throwing a fit, thanks to the sudden bursts of noise and sparks. The horse seemed to be losing her mind and it wasn't long before she reared up and pumped her legs into the air. The instant she dropped back down again, she lashed out with both rear legs.

The wall closest to Willie was no match for the horse's strength and cracked instantly on impact. After a few more bucks, the horse kicked around the same spot until several of the planks simply fell away.

. "All right, Willie," Jake said with surprise. "That's the way!"

Jake got his feet under him and worked his way to the rampaging horse. As he sidestepped in that direction, he fired a few more quick shots at the men huddled by the front door. He didn't even bother to look to see if any of his shots had drawn blood. Instead, Jake was happy just to get over to Willie's side so he could start calming the horse as best he could.

"Hey!" the shotgunner hollered. "Where do you think you're going?"

Jake was patting Willie's mane and rubbing the horse's neck while making the first attempt to lift a foot into the stirrups.

By now, the bigger cowboy had flopped over to sit with his back against the wall. From there, he was able to lift his pistol and take aim at Jake. Unlike the first time he'd fired, the cowboy's eyes were now filled with a murderous gleam that only pain could bring.

The cowboy fired his pistol and missed his target by a matter of inches. It was plenty close enough, however, to make it that much more difficult for Jake to climb into the saddle.

"It's all right, Willie," Jake said in a hurried whisper. "Just let me climb on and we'll be out of here in no time."

If Willie hadn't been paying attention before, the horse sure as hell was listening now. In fact, she seemed to have a very good comprehension of the language, since she held still just long enough for Jake to climb into the saddle. After that, those hooves began pounding against the floor again.

Jake pointed the horse's nose to the wall that was already busted and snapped the reins. To cover his exit as well as give Willie a little more incentive, Jake fired his last bullet at the two cowboys. That sent the horse charging forward to easily break out of the shack.

"Son of a bitch!" the shotgunner yelled as he emptied his last barrel at the horse's rump. But Willie was already off and running, so the buckshot buried itself into what was left of the back wall.

NINETEEN

Although he could see some lights and movement coming from Hendricks, Clint was too far away to hear any of the noise that went along with it. If he closed his eyes, he could imagine the hollering and music that usually drifted out of any saloon. Then again, with the peace and quiet surrounding the Learner place, there wasn't much need to imagine anything else.

Just standing there with the cool darkness enveloping him was enough to take his mind off the stitches that were like hungry gnats nibbling at his skin. The knife wound itself was causing him a dull throbbing pain and was easily overlooked.

"Are you coming inside?" Amelia asked as she stepped onto the porch.

"In a bit. I was just getting some fresh air. Helps the food settle."

"With all you ate, you might need to sleep out here to get enough fresh air to do that job."

"Good point."

Amelia took a few more steps until she was standing beside him. Crossing her arms, she gazed up at the stars while slowly leaning back until her shoulders were against his chest. "I never get sick of looking at that sky."

"I know what you mean."

Pulling in a deep breath, Amelia said, "I can smell my father's cigars. Did he make you smoke one with him?"

"I've been through worse."

Turning around to face him, Amelia reached around Clint's waist until her hand came to rest upon the spot where his stitches were. "Hopefully that cigar will be the worst you get for a good, long while."

Clint savored the feel of her hand gently brushing against him. "Me, too," he said while instinctively placing his hand upon her hip. It was an innocent enough gesture, but sent a wave of heat through his body.

Amelia's waist curved nicely under his hand and felt even nicer when she shifted from one foot to another. Being this close to her allowed Clint to catch the scent of her hair as the wind brushed past both of them. The cold brought Amelia even closer, so they could share the heat coming from each other's bodies.

Clint looked into her eyes and saw her stare right back up at him expectantly. Her lips were red and moist as they parted slightly in anticipation.

"Hey!"

The voice hit both of their ears like a gunshot and caused Amelia to jump and reflexively back away. Clint stayed perfectly still, but could feel his heart slam against the inside of his ribs. He let out a breath and turned to see the one who'd broken the moment.

Dave rushed toward the front porch. He was big for his age, but still young enough to carry himself more like a boy than a man. His hair was mussed and a sneaky grin was plastered all over his face.

"What are you doing out here, Amelia?" Dave chided.

Even though she was in her twenties, Amelia sounded

about ten years younger whenever she talked to her little brother. "Just talking to Clint."

"Well, Pa told me to keep an eye on you two."

"Knowing you're lurking in the shadows is plenty to keep anyone in line," Clint said.

Hearing that, Dave straightened up a bit. "You said you're Clint Adams?"

"That's a fact."

"I heard'a you."

"Did you?"

Dave nodded. "Folks call you the Gunsmith."

"You heard right. If I had my Colt on me, I could show you a thing or two."

When Dave's eyes widened, he looked even more like a little boy. "No fooling?"

"After I get some rest, I'd be happy to show you a few things I've picked up over the years. Tell you the truth, though," he added, "getting bushwhacked in the dark like this made me pull my stitches."

Dave's jaw dropped a bit and he hopped onto the porch. "Sorry about that. I'll let you have your rest. You promise to show me in the morning?"

"Only if I'm feeling better."

That was all Dave needed to hear to get him hurrying into the house.

"I'll have to remember that trick," Amelia said.

Clint gathered her into his arms and whispered, "I've got some other ones I'd rather show you."

TWENTY

Clint didn't have to wait long before the Learner home was just as quiet as the land surrounding it. Since he'd gotten up at the crack of dawn, Frank was asleep in his bed and snoring loudly enough to wake the dead. Dave had made himself scarce and eventually fallen asleep in a chair in the sitting room.

After checking in on Eclipse, Clint was satisfied that the stallion was doing just fine in the barn next to the house. In fact, Eclipse looked more rested than he'd been in months, thanks to the care Dave had taken in feeding and grooming him. Clint then stepped into the house and found Dave snoring in his chair.

Clint took a few minutes to walk around the house, which was all he needed to realize he'd been sleeping in what had to be Dave's room. Once he figured that out, he went to the front room and dragged Dave to his feet. The boy grumbled incoherently, but came awake enough to stand on his own.

"Wha—? Huh?" Dave muttered.

"Come on," Clint said. "You can have your room back."

"You leaving?"

"No, but I'm feeling well enough to sleep out here."

Dave shook his head and said, "I'm supposed to sleep out here when there's a guest."

"Too late," Clint said as he gave Dave a little shove into his room. "We're already here."

The moment Dave stumbled against his bed, he lowered himself onto it and dozed off immediately. Clint stepped out and shut the door behind him. When he turned to look down the short hallway, he found Amelia standing in her room, looking at him through a half-open door.

"Where have you been?" she whispered.

"Just stretching my legs. Paying a visit to my horse. Usual stuff."

"I was beginning to think you were avoiding me."

Clint walked up to her door and leaned against the frame. "Not hardly. It took my last bit of strength to keep from coming in here before everyone was asleep."

"Why wait so long?" she asked. "Were you planning on making noise?"

Before Clint could answer that question, Amelia opened the door the rest of the way to reveal the black-and-white lace she was wearing.

The corset wrapped around her midsection wasn't anything fancy, but it hugged her body perfectly. Black lace cupped firm, rounded breasts that looked just the right size to be cupped in a man's hands. Her nipples were already getting hard and poking through the material.

A white ruffle ran between her breasts and down her stomach, then joined with the ruffle that encircled the bottom of the corset. Amelia wore a pair of small underpants that matched the corset and had little black ribbons that hung down over the tops of her thighs.

Standing in the doorway, she let Clint's eyes wander over her body. In fact, as the seconds ticked by, she smiled and leaned back as if she could actually feel his gaze moving against her skin. Her dark hair looked especially black in the shadows of the hallway and her skin looked especially pale.

"You look beautiful," Clint said.

She opened her eyes slowly and replied, "Thank you. Would you like to come in?"

Being the only woman in the house, Amelia had the bedroom furthest away from the others. That way, when she let Clint in and shut the door, they couldn't hear so much as a peep from the rest of the house. Once they were both shut inside that room, the rest of the world faded away.

The room was big enough to hold a four-poster bed, a mirror and dresser, a chest of drawers, and a washbasin. A window covered with frilly curtains overlooked the back section of the Learners' property. Amelia stepped up to the window and only had to wait a second or two before Clint was easing in behind her. His hands slipped around her waist and he brushed his face against her hair.

"It's funny," she said quietly. "Right out there was the spot where I found you."

Clint laughed and took a look outside. All he could see was a few shapes in the darkness, but he could picture the pigpen and broken fence easily enough. "Bleeding and laying in the mud. Not what I would call my best entrance."

She leaned back against him and placed her hands on top of Clint's. "I was thinking about this moment right from the start. Even when you were bleeding and laying in the mud." Reaching up with one hand, she brushed her fingers against his face and added, "I always knew you'd clean up pretty good."

"Did you, now?" As he said that, Clint tightened his grip on Amelia and spun her around so she was facing him.

She seemed shy at first, but quickly lifted her chin and smiled as she saw Clint's eyes wander down along the front of her body. Soon, Clint's hands followed along that same trail.

Clint moved his palms along her sides, over her hips, and then back up again so he could feel the sides of her breasts. He lingered there for a while, noticing the way

Amelia breathed deeply until she was sighing contentedly with her eyes closed and her head leaning back.

Slowly, Clint moved his hands until he was cupping her breasts. The longer he did, the closer Amelia moved to him, until her body was pressed against his and her leg was sliding up along his side.

Soon, Clint felt her hands on him. Amelia started by rubbing his chest. Then, she drifted down along his stomach. By the time Clint had eased his own hands down to the small of her back, she was reaching between his legs to rub the growing erection she found there.

"It feels like I've waited for this for so long," she whispered.

Sweeping her up in his arms, Clint carried Amelia to her bed. He laid her down and said, "I won't make you wait one more second."

TWENTY-ONE

Clint started to take his shirt off, but quickly found Amelia leaning forward to finish the job. Her eyes were hungry as she unbuttoned his shirt and peeled it off. The moment she could get her hands on his chest, she was rubbing him and anxious to work her way down.

After unbuckling his pants, she practically ripped them off of him so she could get to what she'd only sampled a few minutes ago. Clint crawled next to her and lay on the bed, allowing Amelia to move her hands over every inch of his body.

The corset was fastened on with a variety of buckles, hooks, and buttons, but Clint got through those without much of a problem. It fell away from her to reveal her pert breasts, capped with little pink nipples. Clint's first instinct was to lean forward and kiss those nipples before brushing them gently against his teeth.

Amelia let out a surprised little moan and moved her hands to the back of Clint's head so he could continue what he was doing. Arching her back, she thrust her breasts forward, savoring the feel of Clint's lips against her sensitive skin. Although she didn't want him to stop, she was quickly satisfied when he placed a row of kisses up to her neck.

Sliding one hand over her buttocks, Clint rolled Amelia onto her back and started tugging at her black-and-white lace bottoms. They came off easily once he unbuttoned her garters so her stockings would remain. Amelia parted her long legs for him, revealing the little thatch of hair between them.

Clint eased his hand along her inner thighs, working his way up until his fingers glided over the lips of her pussy. He could feel her whole body tremble as he rubbed her there. The smooth skin became moist and warm to his touch. Soon, Amelia was breathing heavily and moaning with each exhale.

Her skin was so soft and warm that Clint couldn't help but put his lips on it. He kissed her inner thigh and nibbled a bit along the way. When he got to the warm spot between her legs, he flicked his tongue and teased the nub of her clitoris.

Amelia's eyes shot open and her fingers tightened around the back of his head. She looked down at him while biting her lower lip in an effort to keep herself from crying out. The more Clint licked her, the more she bit down. Soon, she felt the pulse of an orgasm brewing under the spot where his tongue was touching her.

Feeling the way her body squirmed and shook, Clint kept up what he was doing until Amelia arched her back with a powerful climax. By the time he crawled on top of her, she was breathless and lying with the side of her face against her pillow.

Clint used one finger to turn her chin so she was facing him. He looked into her eyes and asked, "You doing all right?"

"Better than I've ever been." When she said that, her voice was strong and insistent. Her hands were even more so as she took hold of his hard cock and guided it between her legs. When he was inside of her, she spread her legs wide and took him all the way in.

Clint slid easily into her. Amelia was wet and ready for him. She let out a slow breath that didn't end until he filled her completely. Clint supported himself on one elbow, freeing up his other hand to feel Amelia's naked skin beneath him.

Her nipples were rigid and sensitive. Her hips wriggled invitingly against his palm as he pumped in and out of her. She enveloped him tightly, wrapping around his cock as if to massage it with every thrust. Clint soon found his hands cupping her tight backside. That way, he could pull her in close as he pumped into her.

Amelia leaned back and savored the feel of him moving inside of her. She dragged her fingernails along Clint's bare shoulders and entwined one leg around his. Her other leg was propped up on the bed so she could begin pumping her own hips in time to his rhythm.

After burying himself all the way inside of her, Clint stopped moving and looked down at Amelia's face. She had her eyes clenched shut and her lips slightly parted. The moment she opened them, Clint kissed her passionately on the lips and pushed just a bit more into her.

That extra little push was enough to push Amelia over the edge one more time. She clenched tightly around the shaft of his penis as another orgasm rolled through her body. When she let out her moan, it went directly into Clint's mouth. That breath was accompanied by her tongue, which mingled with his own.

Locked in that kiss, Clint kept moving his hips from side to side while savoring the way Amelia's body trembled underneath him. He didn't pull out of her more than an inch or so before driving straight in again. He could tell by the way she grabbed onto him and dug her nails into his back that he was on the right track.

Amelia's orgasm took its time moving through her. When it passed, it left her breathless and weak. Even so, she came to life again the moment she felt Clint's rigid penis shifting inside of her.

He slid in and out of her slowly at first. Before long, he saw the fire ignite in her eyes once more and felt the way her hands and hips urged him to go faster. That was more than enough to get him going again. Her pussy was still tight around his cock and sent a chill down Clint's back as he thrust in and out of it.

Raising himself up onto his knees, Clint took hold of her hips in both hands and grabbed her tightly. Every time he thrust into her, he did it with a little more power. As he started pulling her hips toward him, Clint didn't feel the least bit of resistance from Amelia.

She had a hold of her pillow and watched him as if she was hanging on for her life. Every time he slammed into her, she let out a soft moan and her eyes grew wide. Soon, she was smiling and leaning back as Clint continued to pump between her legs.

When he felt his own orgasm approaching, Clint pulled Amelia's body into him and drove forward one more time. He buried himself completely in her and felt his own pleasure reach its peak. Amelia squirmed and writhed beneath him, savoring the moment just as much as Clint.

TWENTY-TWO

Hendricks was a town originally built at the end of a cattle drive. To be more precise, it was built where one drive ended and another began, as a herd from western Nebraska was brought all the way down into Texas. The drive was split, thanks to an arrangement between two ranchers, and the cowboys didn't take it upon themselves to argue. They were happy just to reach a place where they could spend their money and drink some whiskey. Hendricks was more than happy to oblige.

Like many other cow towns, Hendricks made most of its money on saloons. Between the alcohol poured there, the women who worked there, and the games that were played at its tables, it was a strike that overshadowed most of those found by hopeful miners who scraped their living out of Nevada's rocks and rivers.

That sort of upbringing normally made a town fairly rowdy. With the saloons practically paying for every inch of boardwalk in Hendricks, the town embraced its rowdiness with a passion. The girls sat with their legs dangling from balconies, giving the occasional passerby on the street a quick, free show. Fights were all but encouraged as a way to boost a certain saloon's reputation.

It was the sort of place that kept men like Frank Learner away. In fact, Frank couldn't have steered further away from that town if it was on fire. Sometimes, however, he was forced to grit his teeth and ride into Hendricks.

He did so this morning, driving his small cart to one of the stores that he frequented simply because it was closest to the outskirts of the town. The old man running that store had the same sour look on his face as Frank. After all, he'd built his store on the outskirts for the same reason that men like Frank went there.

"Hey there, Earl," Frank grunted as he stepped down from his cart.

Earl was older than the hills and had a face that looked like the cracked floor of a desert. He responded to Frank's greeting with a quick, upward nod while lifting himself out of the chair that was situated just outside his shop.

"How's things?" Frank asked.

Earl walked with his back stooped and shoved open the store's front door as if he was angry at it. "Same as always. Bunch of assholes filled with piss and vinegar treating this place like their own personal shit hole."

Frank couldn't help but laugh at the old coot. Earl was one of the few people who made Frank look like a ray of sunshine in comparison. "Same as always, huh?"

"Nah. This bunch ain't with any drive. They just came in and set up shop down the street." When he said that, Earl nodded toward the Copperhead Saloon.

"Rough bunch?"

Earl shuffled into his store and said, "Place is named after a snake, so just the snakes go there."

"What have they been doing that's so bad?"

"Starting fights and screaming like banshees, for one. For another . . . eh, they're just assholes."

So far, Frank didn't hear much of anything that would distinguish those new cowboys from any of the others that had come through town. But arguing with Earl was a lost cause, so he just let it lay.

"What about you?" Earl grunted. "How are those kids of yours?"

"Just fine. Amelia found herself a stray."

"Huh?"

"Some fella wound up in my pigpen. He was hurt."

"Hurt, how?"

"Stabbed."

"Jesus," Earl grunted. "These animals never stop ripping pieces off each other. Serves 'em all right, I suppose. Maybe someday they'll do the world a favor and stay down when they fall."

"Yeah, maybe."

"Better watch that little daughter of yours. If that fella gets a look at her, she might be in a bit of trouble. How old's she, anyways? Fifteen? Sixteen?"

"Add on about seven years."

Earl's eyes widened a bit as he took a moment to consider that. He shook his head in disbelief and grunted, "Time flies. I guess she can take care of herself, then."

Now, Frank was staring at the wall behind Earl's head. His eyes narrowed as he thought more about what was being said.

"Where'd that fella get off to?" Earl asked. "He over at the doc's place?"

"No. Amelia stitched him up and I let him rest at my place."

"I suppose you know your own business, but I wouldn't be so quick to leave any man around a daughter as pretty as yours. That boy still around? He's got to be old enough to have some muscle on his bones."

"He's just a few years behind Amelia."

"Well, that's good, at least," Earl said with a nod. "He knows well enough to keep an eye on his sister."

That made Frank's eyes narrow even more until he

seemed ready to burn a hole through Earl's wall with his stare.

"That fella behaving himself?" Earl asked.

"Near as I can tell."

"Well, if not, there's plenty of assholes with guns around here looking for someone to shoot."

"What was that?"

"You know," Earl replied. "Like I said before. Have these young punks rip at each other until we're rid of 'em. Maybe then we could have some peace and quiet around here."

Frank let out a sigh and shook his head. "Amelia can handle herself and Dave's got the man's gun."

"Oh, then you should be fine. What can I get for you, Frank? Either buy something or move on. I ain't got all day to flap my gums."

TWENTY-THREE

It was a dreary day as a patch of rain clouds rolled in to block out the sun. Frank was gone and Amelia was off doing some work around the house. Clint's back was hurting him, but not from the stab wound or the stitches. Most of the pain came from a cramp that was put there after sleeping in a chair in the sitting room.

As much as he would have liked to stay in Amelia's bed, Clint knew that wouldn't go over too well with Frank. And since he was still a guest in the man's home, he figured it best not to upset the older man too much if he could help it.

The one person that Clint had been concerned about was Dave. The young man had eyed him suspiciously from the moment Clint had woken up that morning. During a quick breakfast, Dave still watched Clint like a hawk. Finally, as Clint was checking in on Eclipse, Dave made his move.

"You're not going to leave, are you?" Dave asked with a definite edge in his voice.

Clint was brushing the stallion's coat as he looked over and shook his head. "Not until I'm done with this."

"You can't leave."

"Why?"

"Because you said you were going to show me how to use a gun."

Considering what he thought the boy might have been about to say, Clint was relieved to hear what had truly been on Dave's mind. "I'm fresh out of guns right now," Clint said. Before he could say another word, Clint saw his modified Colt appear in Dave's hand.

"It ain't loaded," Dave said. "But you can show me how to quick draw."

Clint took the gun and flipped open the cylinder to double check. Sure enough, there wasn't a live round to be seen. "All right, then," he said, while tossing the brush he'd been using and walking for the door. "I suppose I can show you a thing or two."

Even though Dave wasn't more than half a foot shorter than Clint, he chased after him like a puppy. "How many men have you killed, Mr. Adams?"

"That's not a polite question to ask," Clint replied. "And it's not something anyone should brag about."

"I hear men in town bragging about that all the time."

"Is that so?"

Dave nodded.

"Where'd you hear that kind of talk?"

"Down at the Copperhead. It's the toughest saloon in Hendricks."

"Does your father know you spend time in there?"

Quickly, Dave lowered his eyes and shook his head. "No, sir. I just like to see if I can find any known men in there."

"And that's where you hear all that bragging?"

"Yes."

"Well, the men who brag like that are idiots. Have you ever heard the saying that those who can, do?"

Dave thought it over and then shook his head. "What's that mean?"

"It means that men who brag are only good at one thing:

talking. The people who can do more than that are too busy doing it to stand around shooting the breeze in saloons."

"But I've seen fights in the streets outside them places," Dave explained. "I've seen men gun each other down."

"Anyone with some fingers and a thumb can hold a gun and pull a trigger. Hell, I even knew a man missing a few fingers who could still fire a gun. That's nothing to brag about. That's not the sort of man anyone should want to be."

Dave lowered his eyes and shifted his feet. There wasn't any meanness in his face, just an excitement that came from reading too many dime novels. Because of that, Clint cut his preaching short and took his gun belt from where it had been coiled up near Eclipse's stall. He then dropped the gun into the holster and squared his shoulders.

"Watch closely, now," Clint said.

Dave stepped back and watched.

Standing his ground with his eyes narrowed and his hand over the Colt's grip, Clint let out a breath and flexed his fingers. He then twitched his shoulders and flicked his arm less than an inch toward his gun.

"Did you see it?" Clint asked.

"See what?"

"Only the quickest draw known to man!"

Dave's head snapped back and he looked back and forth between Clint's face and hand. After a few seconds, he rolled his eyes and shrugged. "I ain't gonna fall for that."

"All right, then. Try this on for size." Saying that, Clint plucked the Colt from its holster and pointed it at a spot on the barn's wall. He lowered the gun back into its place before snapping it out again at twice the speed. This time, Dave's reaction was completely different.

"Holy cow! I bet you could outdraw any man alive!"

Clint shrugged, drew the Colt, and then spun it around his trigger finger before holstering it again. "I'm not the sort to brag, so maybe you can do it for me."

"Let's see that again!"

After drawing the Colt once more, Clint gave it another couple of spins and then dropped it back into place. He then caught Dave's eye, did one last draw, and handed the gun over. "I suppose your father would prefer that you hold onto that for now."

"Yeah, he would."

"I did craft that pistol myself, though, and would like to know where it's kept. You know, just in case I need it." When he saw a bit of reluctance on Dave's face, Clint added, "You can keep the bullets I gave you and I'll even teach you a trick, besides."

After less than two seconds of contemplation, Dave nodded. "There's a loose board in the back porch. That's where I hide it."

"And that's where it'll stay once we're done. Now, then. Let's see if you can learn a twirl I know. It's a favorite of Buffalo Bill Cody, himself."

TWENTY-FOUR

The gun tricks kept Clint busy for a good portion of the day. They also showed him that he wasn't as ready as he'd thought he was to pack up and leave. Just going through the simple motions of twirling the gun and dropping it into his holster made his skin strain against his stitches. Resting didn't help either, since anything more than sitting was straining his stitches.

It turned out that whoever had been holding that knife couldn't have picked a better spot if they'd tried, without killing him. He knew well enough that climbing into the saddle was the best way possible to rip that wound open and spill a fresh batch of blood onto the ground.

Since he wasn't about to walk out of Hendricks, Clint figured he'd stay on a bit. He spent the rest of that day and a good portion of the next taking it easy around the Learner place and helping out where he could. In his spare time, he managed to teach Dave enough to become something of a decent draw. His reverse twirl needed a bit of work, but that wasn't the sort of thing any self-respecting gunman ever used, anyway. Those tricks were just that: tricks to pass the time. The only time Clint ever used them was to while away a few minutes when there wasn't anything else better to do.

As the sun was setting and the Learners were in town, Clint leaned against the back of the barn and watched the goings-on in Hendricks. Although he couldn't see much more than a few bodies moving here and there, he was starting to get an itch that had nothing to do with his stitches.

Just then, he spotted a body moving a hell of a lot closer than those in town and shifted toward it as his hand dropped reflexively toward the empty space where his holster normally was.

"Jesus, Clint. You look like hell."

"I might say the same thing about you, Jake, but you never did look too good."

Jake walked toward him wearing a tired smile. His face was smeared with dirt and his hands were caked with it as well. "I thought you were dead," Jake said.

"It wasn't from lack of trying. Those cowboys tore after me like I killed their dog. You have any idea why that might be?"

Without responding to that question, Jake walked up to lean against the wall beside him. The moment his shoulders touched against the boards, Jake let out a grateful sigh. "This is the most rest I've gotten in days."

"Pardon my manners, but what the hell are you doing here?"

Jake looked at Clint as if he wasn't going to answer that question. Then, once he got a good helping of the fire in Clint's eyes, he thought better about that. "I've been hiding out not too far from here. I would have come for you earlier, but I truly did think you were dead."

Clint took a step away from the wall. Even though he didn't have his gun on him, he didn't have too much trouble causing Jake to back off a step or two just by glaring at him. "All of this was supposed to be about you pissing off a few cowboys. If you tell me that's still all there is, I swear I'll put you through this wall."

"I thought this was just about my misunderstanding over that card game." Flinching at a movement from Clint, he added, "All right, there was more than one dust-up over cards. When I asked for your help, I swear I didn't know things would go this far."

"Then how'd they wind up like this? Nobody goes through so much trouble just to pay back some loose talk over a card game."

Jake nodded and squirmed as though he had something he wanted to say, but just couldn't get the words to leave his mouth. Finally, he sucked in a breath and let it out. He didn't look a whole lot better after that, but he was able to start talking.

"Somehow, those cowboys must have found out about what I was carrying."

"You mean the money?" Clint asked.

Jake winced and opened his mouth as if he was about to say something. The actual words, however, seemed to have stuck in the back of his throat.

"I know there's got to be more than the money," Clint said. "I was hoping you'd just come out and tell me. Since that chance is gone, don't make me pull it out of you."

"All right. There is more than the money."

"Go on."

"I was hired to carry a few letters to an office in Sacramento."

"If this doesn't speed up, I'm going to have to start pulling."

"They're letters to a railroad planning office," Jake said quickly. "From one of their scouting branches in Pennsylvania. It's actually a report of where the next line should be built."

"All right."

"I don't know how anyone else found out about it, but

the news got leaked somewhere along the way and you can see what kind of hell has broken loose."

"Maybe my head's still a little cloudy, but I don't see why a bunch of cowboys would be interested in some letters between railroad offices."

"That's what I'm trying to tell you," Jake said. "Those cowboys shouldn't give a rat's ass about those letters. When I was hired for this job, I was sworn to secrecy, but that was mainly to keep land barons and the like away from those documents."

When he heard that, Clint felt one of the major pieces fall into place. "Land barons?"

Jake nodded.

"You mean those letters are plotting out where the next set of tracks will be laid down?"

Jake nodded quicker this time, seeing that Clint was catching on to what he was trying to say.

"So if someone had those letters, they'd know which land to buy so they could get rich when the railroad starts bidding on it?"

"You got it. I was told to keep those letters safe and out of sight. The men who gave them to me said there would be some dangerous sorts after that information. Hired guns and the like, but I've been able to avoid all of them. I made it this far without so much as a hiccup."

"That is, until you bit off more than you could chew at that card game," Clint pointed out.

"Well . . . yeah. Even so, I don't know how anyone could have figured out who I was or what I was carrying."

"Men with enough money to buy up enough land to put a squeeze on the railroads can afford to put plenty of ears to the ground."

"Very true. I just never thought that cowboys like those would be anywhere close to that league."

Clint fixed his eyes on Jake and said, "Cowboys generally work for someone. And the men who own cattle driving companies, ranches, or those sorts of businesses tend to run in the very circles you were warned against."

Jake stared straight ahead as that rolled through his mind. The more it sunk in, the paler he got. "Aw, Jesus. How could I be so stupid? I should've known better than that."

"Yes, you should have."

"What am I gonna do? There could be any number of hired guns headed this way!"

"Does anyone know you're here?"

"I was holed up a few miles away and was ambushed. I got away clean. I know that for certain."

"Which means they'll probably be looking for you and watching all the roads leading out of town. It'd be best for you to lay low and keep your head down until we find a safe route out of here."

"Do you think you could help me look?" Dave asked. "You got me this far and there's not much farther for me to go."

"Sacramento is a ways off," Clint pointed out.

"Not compared to how far I've already come. Please, Clint. I wouldn't have made it this far without you."

"You've made it plenty far on your own."

"But that was all a lot of riding, which I can do with my eyes shut. Things are getting tough now and I need backup before someone gets hurt."

Clint glared at Jake a little harder, but it still took the courier a few seconds to realize what the look was for.

"Well," Jake added, "before someone gets hurt more. There's no good reason for you to help me, Clint. But I'm asking you all the same."

"Tell you what. I'll help, but I want to help you all the way to Sacramento."

"That'd be perfect!"

"That means you listen to what I say, do what I tell you, and introduce me to your bosses when it's done."

"Ah, you want to be paid."

"Considering I'm the one that's gotten stabbed and I'm the one that will be putting my neck on the line, I'd say that's fair."

Jake nodded and grinned. "The men who hired me have more than enough to make this job worth your while."

"We'll just see about that."

TWENTY-FIVE

The Bella Donna was the only place in Hendricks that didn't cater to cowboys who'd come into a chunk of money. It was a gambling club and restaurant that catered to those who already had their money and wouldn't be parting with it anytime soon. The inside was decorated with imported carpets and drapes. The tables were solid oak and the brass rails on the bars were polished daily.

It was a small place, but made enough from occasionally renting out its high-end rooms upstairs to pay to keep it up and running until the next big spender came along. There were big men working the doors whose only job was to keep out the riffraff that made up most of the town's population. They immediately reached for their guns when they saw the two cowboys walk up to the front door.

"Whiskey's too expensive for you boys in there," one of the monsters in silk vests said. "Try the Copperhead down the street."

"Already been there," Red said. "I got word that I'm to meet someone in here."

"Meet who?"

"Mr. Cumberland."

Both of the guards shot glances to each other before

nodding. "My partner will check on it," the first one said while the second ducked into the building. "Wait here."

It only took a minute for the second guard to reappear and nod to the first.

"All right," the first one said. "Go on in. But don't break anything, or we'll break you to make up for it."

Normally, Red had a comment ready and raring to go when he heard something like that. This time, however, he was facing a man who looked less like a man and more like a brick wall with a silk vest draped over it. To this man, Red tipped his hat and moved along.

Red stopped for a moment to take in the refined elegance of the Bella Donna. It was the sort of elegance that even the lowest of cretins could admire. The place even smelled fancy.

While Red was still gaping at the scenery, he heard a voice coming from one of the nearby parlors. "You're the man Mr. Cumberland is waiting for?"

"I am."

"Come along with me. I'm the owner of this establishment."

The owner was a refined man in his fifties who'd come all the way over from London. He was wearing a broad smile on this day because he'd just checked in a customer who would keep his establishment open for another couple of months.

"Mr. Cumberland is right in there," the owner said as he swept his arm toward a set of polished double doors.

Red pushed the doors open and stepped into a dark, paneled room with a small bar on one end and a set of three matching card tables taking up most of the floor. A phonograph played the music of a string quartet as a large man wearing a pearl-gray suit sat with a working girl in his lap at the furthest table.

"There you are, Red. So good to finally meet you."

Red took his hat off and held it in both hands. He didn't

know why he did that, exactly, apart from the fact that it seemed the proper thing to do under the circumstances. "Mr. Cumberland?"

"That's me. Come over here and have a seat."

Once Red came around to the other side of the table, he heard a dull slap and saw the working girl jump off of Cumberland's lap.

"Time for us to talk business, darling," Cumberland said. "Just wait right over there until we're done."

Unlike most women in the world, this one didn't mind being addressed or swatted like a fly. Of course, most other women weren't paid so much just to look pretty and smile at the richest men in the room. This woman was doing her job exceptionally well.

Cumberland was a big man with a thick handlebar mustache and thick black hair. He had a solid build and a suit that was so well made that it hung on him without straining at a single seam. He didn't wear a gun, but it was plain to see that the only other man in the room was there to do that for him.

"You want a drink?" Cumberland asked.

"Um, no. Maybe later."

"There won't be a later because I'm going to make this quick. My associate was promised by your employer that you knew the whereabouts of a certain Jake McKean."

"Yes, sir, we do."

"Then where is he?"

"We almost had him not too long ago, but he got away."

"So you don't know where he is," Cumberland stated.

Red wasn't accustomed to squirming, but he found himself doing just that when he heard the biting tone in Cumberland's voice. "Me and my crew have been watching this town and all the trails to and from it. We know he was supposed to deliver his package here, so—"

"He was supposed to make a stop here," Cumberland snipped. "He was supposed to stop in here and meet with a representative from the railroad so he could check in. He hasn't shown up yet."

"If you know that much, then maybe you could—"

"Could what?" Cumberland asked with a growl in the back of his throat. "Follow him myself? Track him down on my own? Do the job that you were supposed to do?"

"All I was going to say is—"

"Whatever it is, save it. I know you were brought in on this a little late, which is why I'm cutting you as much slack as I am. That courier needs to be found. I need to get a look at what he's carrying and then he needs to be sent on his way. All of this needs to happen without there being any connection to me or my associates. Is that understood?"

"Yes, sir."

"Do you think you can handle this job or should I find someone else?"

"Me and my boys can do it," Red insisted. "But there's someone else riding with that courier. A gunman."

"Is he employed by the railroads or the courier service?"

Red thought about that for a few moments, then shook his head. "I don't think so. He just met up with Jake during a card game."

"Then he can fill a hole in the desert for all I care. Now get the hell out of here and don't come back until you've got that package for me to examine."

TWENTY-SIX

When the cart returned from town, Dave was the first one to jump off. Frank waited for it to stop and then climbed down to help his daughter. By this time, Clint had already walked up to them and was circling around to the back of the rickety vehicle.

"Riding into town twice in one day?" Clint asked. "And here I had you folks pegged for the quiet type."

Frank pulled down the back of the cart and slapped a small stack of sacks. "We had to go in twice today so we wouldn't have to go back later. You feeling well enough to carry any of these?"

"Don't ask Clint to do that," Amelia said. "Remember his stitches?"

"I can at least try," Clint responded. "I'd feel too guilty just standing back while you do all the work."

Frank nodded and pulled one of the sacks from the cart. "Turn around," he grunted to Clint.

Clint did as he was told and stood with his wound facing away from the cart. Without much by way of a warning, Frank set one of the sacks onto Clint's shoulder.

"You got it?" the older man asked.

Clint could feel the skin straining against his stitches,

106

but didn't feel any of it about to tear. "Where do these need to go?"

Pointing to the barn which wasn't more than a dozen paces away, Frank said, "Right over there."

"Then I've got it."

Clint, Frank, and Dave unloaded the cart with ease and headed for the house. Amelia was standing outside and allowed her father and brother to walk past her before stepping in Clint's way. She stopped him with a hand against his chest and let it linger just long enough to feel his body underneath his shirt.

"I hope you didn't hurt yourself," she whispered.

"Nah. I'm healing up pretty good."

"So I guess you'll be moving on soon?"

"Actually, I was going to ask if I could stay for just a little bit longer. Maybe just another day or—"

"That would be wonderful!" Amelia said quickly. "I was hoping you wouldn't rush off." Lowering her voice again, she added, "I was also hoping we could have some more time together. Last time was . . ."

She let that trail off when the front door swung open and Frank stuck his head outside. "You gonna cook supper, Amelia, or are we gonna starve to death?"

Amelia wasn't even affected by Frank's coarse tone and simply tossed her father a quick nod. "Clint needs to stay with us for a bit longer. That's all right, isn't it?"

Frank's eyes narrowed and he locked his gaze upon Clint. After a few long seconds, he shrugged and said, "I guess. Maybe I can fix up a proper bed for him in the barn." With that, Frank stepped back inside and let the door slam shut.

"I don't think your father likes me very much," Clint said.

"Oh, he was just kidding. Stay as long as you like."

"Come to think of it, maybe I should rent a room in town."

She grabbed hold of his hands and shook her head. "This is my house too and I want you to stay."

"It's not about that. It's just that . . . well . . . you know how I came to be here. The men that were after me may still be around. I wouldn't want to draw any attention to you or your family."

Amelia's face darkened a bit and she let go of his hands. "Oh. That's different. I thought they weren't anywhere near here."

"That's what I thought, too. It seems they may still be around and if we cross paths again, I doubt it'll be pretty."

"I'd hate to send you out before you're healed."

"I'm doing pretty good. You took real good care of me, so now let me take care of you in return."

Judging by the smile that came onto her face, Amelia liked the sound of that. "All right," she said as she reached out and brushed her hand along the side of Clint's arm. "But I'd like to see you again before you leave town altogether."

"Maybe I could come back for dinner. You're one hell of a cook."

"And Dave will want to try to get some more gun-fighting stories out of you."

"Naturally."

"And promise me you'll be careful no matter what happens."

"Hey," Clint said with a grin. "I wouldn't have made it this long any other way."

TWENTY-SEVEN

Jake crouched down so low as he walked that he might have been more comfortable crawling. He kept his hands stretched out in front of him to run along the top of the weeds that sprouted out from the ground behind Sixth Street. It was the time of night where it was as dark and loud as Hendricks could get.

He figured it was the perfect time to slip in and out of town unseen.

He was wrong.

Just as Jake caught sight of his horse tied up behind a row of buildings, he heard the distinct crunch of boots against gravel. Those boots were much too close for comfort, so Jake sped up his own pace toward the waiting horse.

He held his breath for the next couple of steps, praying that he could make it to his saddle without getting stopped. That way, no matter whose boots were making that noise, Jake could get away from there.

His horse had been tied to an old hitching post at the back end of an alley. By the looks of it, that post had been there ever since a real street had run along the back of that alley. Now, there was nothing but an empty lot that looked out on a few less-empty lots.

Jake's hand drifted instinctively toward the gun stuck under his belt as the crunch of gravel echoed through the air. The next thing he heard was a gruff voice as a powerful hand slammed down upon his shoulder.

"You're a slippery little bastard, Jake," Red said as he stepped out from a shadow not too far from Jake's horse.

But Red wasn't the one who'd grabbed hold of Jake. That hand belonged to one of the other cowboys that Jake had started to see in his nightmares.

Since he didn't have to ask what the cowboys wanted, Jake assumed the worst and acted on it. Both of his hands grabbed hold of the hand on his shoulder to keep it in place. From there, Jake twisted his head around and sunk his teeth into the meaty portion between the cowboy's thumb and forefinger.

Harry let go as if Jake was a hot coal and screamed in pain as blood gushed from his hand. Jake didn't release him right away, which ripped open the bite wound that much more.

"Little bastard," Red snarled as he drew his gun and took aim. Unfortunately, his barrel was pointed straight at the face of his partner by the time his finger touched the trigger. Red managed to ease up before accidentally blowing Harry's head off.

Jake started to run toward his horse, but that way was already cut off, since Red had been standing there with his gun already drawn. So, rather than try to repeat the same tactics he'd used in his last encounter with the cowboys, Jake had to find another route.

When Jake pulled his gun from under his belt, he got the end of the barrel caught on his pants. It took a few desperate tugs, but Jake finally managed to get the gun free.

"Aw, look at that," Red mused. "He's gonna try and shoot it out with us."

But Harry wasn't in the mood for jokes. He flicked some blood from his bitten hand just as a fresh batch of crimson flowed out to cover it again. "I'm gonna shoot that fucking prick and be done with it."

"No!"

During the course of this conversation, Jake saw Red's gun twitch away from him just long enough to give him a bit of courage. He quickly aimed at the cowboy and pulled his trigger. The gun barked down the alley and sent a plume of smoke rolling through the air.

"Don't let him get away!" Red shouted.

Harry didn't need to be told twice. He was already bolting after Jake like he'd been launched from a cannon. As Harry ran, he whistled loudly enough for the other two cowboys to hear him from across the street.

Red shifted his aim and fired off a shot of his own, which dug into a wall half a second after Jake had passed it. He couldn't take a second shot since his line of fire was once again blocked by Harry.

Before he took off after the group, Red walked over to Jake's horse and put his gun to the animal's head. "I bet Jake would be real brokenhearted if he found you laying in a heap."

Jake's horse was chewing on some of the nearby weeds and barely even glanced at Red while going through those motions.

"Eh, I don't like to hurt no animal. But you may have something I need." With that, Red flipped open the saddlebags and felt around inside. He also slipped his hand underneath the saddle itself and pulled out a thin leather envelope.

Red's eyes widened at the sight of it, but all he found was a few folded bills. He took the money anyway, tossed the envelope, and ran down the alley.

TWENTY-EIGHT

Jake ran for his life, clutching his gun in hand and bolting for the other side of the street. He took a shot or two over his shoulder, but stopped when he almost ran straight into someone standing on the corner. That someone drew his gun, took aim, and fired.

The shot blasted past Jake's head and tore a chunk out of Harry's shoulder. Harry spun on one heel, let out a shriek, and sent his gun skidding against the dirt.

For a moment, Jake could only stand there and look at the familiar face. Then he couldn't keep from talking.

"Clint, I'm so glad to see you! There's a few more of them somewhere and at least one of them back by my horse."

Clint reached out to push Jake to one side and sighted along the barrel of his Colt. "I know. I can see them."

"You saved my life, Clint. Saved it again!"

"I know, I was there. If you don't shut up and get out of my way, you'll have to save your own skin for a change!"

Jake nodded quickly and stepped aside to clear Clint's line of sight. At that moment, Red came storming out of the alley with his gun held out in front of him. Clint fired

112

off a pair of quick shots, each one of them getting closer to Red's cheek than the last.

As the lead whipped by him, Red jumped back so quickly that he nearly lost his balance. He fired off a round or two before hitting the back of his heel against a crooked board on the boardwalk and going down. Another pair of cowboys rushed out to his side, but didn't seem so anxious to help him up.

"I'm getting sick of seeing you boys," Clint said. "Last time, I took a knife in the back. Right about now, I'm having a hard time thinking of a reason not to gun you all down out of self-defense."

There was a moment where Clint thought that was all he'd need to say to chase them off. Then, one of the cowboys made a bad move and raised his gun.

Clint shifted on his heels, squeezed his trigger, and sent a bullet straight through that cowboy's skull.

After that, the rest of the men couldn't run away fast enough.

When he saw Jake lift his gun and take aim at one of the fleeing men, Clint shoved the man's gun hand toward the sky. Jake's pistol barked once and sent its payload toward the stars.

"What the hell?" Jake exclaimed. "I had a clear shot."

"Yeah, at a man's back."

"They're trying to kill us, unless you haven't noticed."

"And, in case you haven't noticed, they're doing a piss-poor job of trying to kill us. It'll take more than that for me to feel comfortable with seeing a man get shot in the back."

Jake let out a sigh and watched as Red and his cowboys scattered in a couple different directions. For the moment, every single one of those directions was away from where he and Clint were standing.

"I suppose you're right," Jake said. "I just thought we'd

be justified, seeing as how they're shooting at us and one of them stabbed you."

"Justified by some, maybe. Not by me." Uninterested in whatever arguments Jake was about to make, Clint walked over to the cowboy that had been killed and used his boot to roll the body onto its back. "You recognize that man?"

Jake managed to look at the corpse for less than a second before turning away. "Aw, Jesus. I was trying not to look at that."

"I was just trying to find a clean hotel for the night, so I didn't exactly want to see this either. Besides, you were about to put a bullet in a man's back, so you should be able to stomach a bit of blood."

Jake looked down and shook his head.

"Are you sure?" Clint asked. "Take a good look."

Once more, Jake looked down. This time was a bit easier to handle than the first and he actually managed to look long enough to pick out some of the dead man's features under all that blood. Just to be certain, he squatted down a bit and took a closer look. Jake then stood up and shook his head. "Nope. I've never seen that man before."

"You certain?"

Jake nodded.

"What about at that card game? Did you see him anywhere around the table or even at the saloon? Maybe sometime after I left?"

Rolling his eyes up to the tops of their sockets, Jake held them there as if the memories he was seeking were being played just over his head. After a few more seconds, he looked back down to Clint and said, "Nope."

"I know I haven't seen him before, so that means that cowboy you pissed off either has a lot of friends or he's getting reinforcements from somewhere."

"You really think so?"

Clint fixed a stare on Jake and replied, "If what you told me about those documents is true, I wouldn't be surprised if these cowboys were just meant to keep us busy until the real gunmen arrive."

"But the men in Sacramento will be suspicious if I don't arrive there with these documents. Doesn't that mean they need me to stay in one piece?"

"Have those men in Sacramento met you before?"

"No."

"Did anyone write down a description of you that they were passing along?"

"Not that I know of."

"Then all they need is for some courier to arrive with those documents at something close to the designated time."

The hope that had been building on Jake's face quickly melted away. "Damn. What the hell do we do now?"

"I can tell you what we're not going to do and that's sit around to wait while a posse of gunmen come our way."

"So you're still with me?" Jake asked with the hope returning to his eyes.

"Sure. It's been a while since I've been to Sacramento, anyway."

TWENTY-NINE

Clint and Jake circled the town for a bit just to make certain that nobody was following in their tracks. Although it was too dark for them to see much, that also meant it was a perfect time for them to slip out of Hendricks without being noticed.

"Come on," Clint said as he and Jake were riding toward the edge of town. "We can put a few miles behind us before we make camp and then strike out in earnest tomorrow."

"We can't do that just yet," Jake said.

"What?"

"I need to meet up with someone from the company that hired me."

"What the hell for?"

"They meet up with me every so often at checkpoints," Jake explained. "The report I told you about is in pieces and this is how I've been collecting it. It's also how they make sure I'm on schedule."

"You never told me the report was in pieces."

"I wasn't supposed to tell you about the report at all! I wasn't supposed to tell anyone. I guess I'm still in the habit of keeping the secret."

"Yeah," Clint grunted. "Too bad you weren't in that habit more often or you wouldn't be in this mess."

Jake shrugged, but kept quiet. There really wasn't much he could say in his own defense.

"How many more stops do you need to make?" Clint asked.

"This is the last one. From here on, I guess the men who write those reports can take them into California on their own."

"And when's the meeting to get this last part?"

"Tomorrow. That's the real reason I've had to stay around this long. I wouldn't blame you if you changed your mind about coming with me."

Clint was pondering that very possibility when Jake said that. Still, despite all the headaches Jake was causing, it boiled down to a difference of hours. What convinced Clint even more was the itching pain in his side where the stitches continued to scrape against his skin.

"I'm still in," Clint said. "The least I can do to pay back the men that have been breathing down our necks is to make sure they don't make a profit from it. But you need to tell me everything from here on in."

"Oh, I will."

"Everything. Understand?"

"Yes I do."

In the time they'd taken to have their conversation, Clint and Jake could already hear more commotion coming from within Hendricks. Looking over his shoulder, Clint could see several people milling about in the vicinity of the shoot-out he'd had with Red and those other cowboys.

"We need to find out who's backing those cowboys' play," Clint said. "Maybe then we'll have a better idea of what else is going to get thrown at us."

"Agreed."

"Maybe I should come along with you for this last meeting."

Jake was shaking his head furiously before Clint even got done talking. "It's supposed to be secret, remember? They don't want anyone else coming with me."

"Fine. I can wait outside."

"I guess you could do that."

With every second that passed, Clint wondered if he should just back out of his agreement and part ways with Jake now before he got something worse than a stab wound to show for it. All he knew for certain was that Jake was headed for one hell of a fall if he rode into Sacramento on his own. Clint didn't know if he could look at himself in a mirror again if he just stepped back and let the man fall.

"Looks like we might have a hard time getting back into town without being noticed," Clint said as he watched more and more people walking the streets of Hendricks. "Do you know somewhere safe to spend the night?"

"I could camp somewhere."

"Actually, you should probably stay with me. I've got a place in mind, but you'll have to keep quiet and stay put until I come to get you."

"You sure about that? I know how to make a camp so's nobody sees it."

"If it's all the same to you, I'd rather have you somewhere I can keep an eye on you and a campsite out in the open isn't what I had in mind."

"Don't you trust me to fend for myself for one night?"

Clint furrowed his brow and replied, "Do you really want me to answer that?"

"Fair enough. Where do you want me to go?"

THIRTY

Clint didn't even have to ride near the few hotels he'd been scouting to see there were men standing or walking in front of each and every one of them. He couldn't be sure any of those men were a cause for concern, but he couldn't be certain that they weren't, either. Since he hadn't seen any of those hotels up close before running into Jake and Red, Clint turned his back on all of them and headed once more to the Learner place.

The house blended well into the darkness and only showed up as a few lighted windows once he got within spitting distance of it. That made it perfect for Clint's purposes. Just to be safe, however, he and Jake circled the property a few times before making their way to the barn.

"You see anyone out there?" Clint asked as he and Jake drew up alongside each other.

"Just a few coyotes. What about you?"

"I didn't even see the coyotes. Let's . . ." He stopped short and held out a hand to point at a shadow that was coming their way.

"Who's out there?" came a familiar voice.

"Take it easy, Dave. It's Clint Adams."

The shadow looked a little bigger than Clint remembered, but that was probably due to the snarling tone that had been forced into the young man's voice. When he spoke again, the boy was more like the one Clint had gotten to know. "Clint? Is that really you?"

"Sure it is. Who'd you think it was?"

As Dave stepped forward, the rifle in his hands was easier to see. It had started to point toward the ground, but came up again when he saw Jake. "Who's that with you?"

"He's a friend of mine, Dave."

"Honest?"

"Yeah. Honest."

After a few more seconds, the boy let out a breath and said, "I thought he might be someone that was after you. I heard there was shooting in town."

"Word travels fast around here," Jake said.

Dave looked up at Jake as if the courier had sprouted horns. "No. I could hear the shooting."

Clint swung down from his saddle and led Eclipse toward the barn. "Is your father or sister around? I need to make sure it's all right that Jake sleeps here tonight."

"It's all right," Dave replied. After he'd let a respectable amount of time go by, he added, "But I'll go check just to make sure."

"Thanks, Dave."

Watching Dave run toward the house, Jake said, "He seems like a good kid. I could have done without that rifle being stuck in my face."

"I'll bet he could outdraw you in a fight," Clint said.

At first, Jake looked over at Clint with confusion. Then he waved off the comment as Clint started laughing under his breath. By this time, Dave was already running out of the house.

"Pa says you might as well stay," the boy shouted.

Even though Dave seemed to have missed the message under the older man's words, Clint could practically hear the hesitant grumble in Frank's voice. "Are you sure about that?"

Just then, the front door swung open and Amelia came running out. "I'm sure," she said. Her smile was bright enough to be seen in the thick shadows and she ran up to Clint as if she was going to jump into his arms. She stopped short after glancing nervously at his wounded side and instead gave him a hug around the neck.

"Glad to see you back so soon," she whispered. "What's the occasion?"

"My friend here needs to meet up with someone tomorrow. After that, we'll be heading into California. We'd sure appreciate a place to stay in the meantime. Something tells me we're going to need all the rest we can get."

"Pa says that other one needs to sleep in the barn," Dave shouted as if Jake was half a mile away.

Jake's eyes widened and he looked over to Clint as if he was the older brother.

"You heard the man," Clint said. "It is his property."

"Oh, come on! I get to sleep in a barn, now?"

Clint walked over to Jake and lowered his voice to a whisper. "These are good folks and I don't want any trouble coming their way. I was going to suggest that one of us sleep out here to make sure nobody tries to ride in and shoot the place up, anyway."

"I guess that makes sense, but why's that got to be me?"

"Because I'm the one with the stab wound and a hundred other things to do that are better than following you across a quarter of the goddamn country."

Clint stared directly into Jake's eyes as those words sunk in. It didn't take long for Jake to nod and say, "You're right."

"And how about this?" Clint added. "The next time we're invited to share the hospitality of a good family, I'll be the one that sleeps in the barn."

Jake was only too eager to stick his hand out. "That's a deal."

Clint pretended not to see the hand Jake was offering. "I'm certain nobody followed us out here, but you've got to keep watch in case someone learns that we're here. You're the one with these cowboys chasing him, so you get that job as well."

"Might as well," Jake grumbled. "Seeing as how I probably won't get much sleep in the damn barn, anyhow."

"That's the spirit." With that, Clint patted Jake on the shoulder and sent him on his way. Amelia was waiting for him in front of the house.

"I hope you don't intend on sleeping in that barn, Clint Adams."

"Not if I can help it."

"Good. Because I've got much better plans for you tonight."

Clint looked over his shoulder at Jake, who was already being questioned by Dave. Some part of Clint actually felt bad for Jake. That part was ignored easily enough, however, once he felt Amelia leading him into the house.

THIRTY-ONE

The meal was a fairly quiet one, even though Jake and
Dave never really stopped talking. The silence came from
Frank, who was churning it out so thick that it was nearly
enough to eclipse all the chatter from the other two. Clint
and Amelia kept their mouths shut and enjoyed their food.
Both of them knew better than to expect much by way of
conversation from the old man.

Once Jake had stuffed down more than twice the
amount of pie Amelia served for dessert, he slapped his
stomach and waddled outside. Despite how fast he tried to
move, he wasn't fast enough to outrun Dave. Frank ex-
cused himself without saying a word, disappeared into his
room, and wasn't heard from again.

"I don't know why my brother's so fascinated with your
friend," Amelia whispered to Clint as they walked down
the hall after everything was cleaned up and squared away.

Shrugging, Clint replied, "Beats me. It might have
something to do with the rumor that Jake used to run from
Indians when he rode with the Pony Express."

"Did he really run from Indians?"

"I doubt it."

"Then how did Dave hear about . . . ?" Amelia didn't

even have to finish that question to know its answer. The guilty smirk on Clint's face was all she needed.

Picking up on the accusation in her eyes, Clint said, "I know your brother likes to hear stories."

She swatted Clint on the arm and shook her head. "You are terrible, Clint Adams. What did Jake ever do to deserve that?"

"Don't get me started on that subject."

Amelia led Clint directly to her own room and stepped inside. Clint stopped at the threshold.

"Should I sleep in Dave's room or in the chair out front?" he asked.

"Neither. You're sleeping with me."

"Should I worry about being killed in my sleep by your father?"

"I'm a grown woman. Or," she added while guiding his hand along the curve of her hip, "hadn't you noticed? Besides, he's already dead asleep."

Clint didn't need to hear another word to convince him. Asking about Frank was more of a formality than a real concern and Amelia's sultry smile was enough to make a preacher think twice about his vows. The fact that Clint knew firsthand what she had in mind for him made his decision even easier.

A few steps forward and Clint was in Amelia's bedroom. He shut the door quietly and turned the lock.

Amelia walked to her bed, turned around, and faced Clint with a warm smile on her lips. She reached back with one hand to pull out the pin that had been holding her hair up and shook it out with a few quick moves of her head.

Watching her, Clint could feel his own body responding until he felt himself moving forward as if his feet were working of their own volition. The moment he was in arm's reach of her, she started pulling open his shirt and unbuckling his pants. When she got to his gun belt, she looked down and smiled.

"Dave was upset when this came up missing," she said.

"He'll get over it," Clint replied as he unbuckled the belt and draped it over a chair.

THIRTY-TWO

Amelia took one step back until she felt her legs bump against the footboard of her bed. She turned to one side and bent at the waist as she unlaced her boots and slid them off her feet. She smiled when she saw how carefully Clint was watching her. She also slowed down her movements to prolong the show.

Slipping her hands beneath her skirt, she slowly straightened up again. Amelia moved her hands around to her back so the front part of her skirt fell down to cover her normally while bunching up at the small of her back.

The disappointment on Clint's face bordered on tragic.

Amelia giggled to herself as she hooked her thumbs into her panties and bent at the waist again to slide them down over her hips and legs. This time, when she stood up, she lifted her skirt as if she was about to cross over a puddle and showed Clint the foot that she used to kick her panties onto the floor.

"That's a nice little trick," Clint said as he moved in closer.

She turned around before he got too close and looked at him over her shoulder. "And that wasn't even the best part," she said. With her back to him, Amelia leaned forward and reached back to take hold of her skirt. Slowly, she lifted her skirt and leaned forward a bit more.

Clint looked down to watch as the bottom of her skirt lifted to show the smooth, creamy skin of her calves and the soft curve of the back of her knee. She lifted the skirt even higher to reveal her finely toned thighs. Her skin seemed to get even smoother as it led from her thighs, up to the gentle curvature of her buttocks.

Now that she had her skirt bunched up at her waist, Amelia held it there and looked once more at Clint over her shoulder. He already had his pants down and one hand on her hip. She was taken by surprise when she felt how hard he was between her legs, but it was most definitely a good surprise.

Clint ran his hand up and down along the curve of her backside. When his hand got near the small of her back, Amelia leaned forward even more and arched her back beautifully. When she spread her legs apart and grabbed hold of the blankets, she felt his hard cock glide between the moist lips of her pussy.

Amelia let out a satisfied moan as he slid all the way into her. That moan took on a bit more of a throaty quality as he drove in even deeper while growing harder by the second. By the time he was fully inside of her, Amelia felt an excited chill working up and down her spine.

Placing both hands on her back, Clint rubbed up as far as he could go before he was blocked by the material of her skirts bunched around her waist. He then moved his hands back down again to the smooth, rounded curves of her buttocks. Taking hold of her firmly, he slid out and then back in with just a bit more speed than he had the first time.

Amelia had hold of her blanket with both hands now. She was making some noise, which sounded like a growl in the back of her throat. Her body was moving impatiently, urging Clint to stop teasing her and do what they both wanted the most.

Unable to control himself any longer, Clint began pumping in and out with increasing momentum. As he pounded into her harder, his hips pressed against her rump and pushed her hard against the bed. Amelia responded to that with a grateful sigh and tossed her hair over her shoulder.

Without missing a beat, Clint reached forward and grabbed hold of as much of her hair as he could in one fist. He pulled her hair just enough for her to crane her head back a bit and then pounded into her once more from behind.

Amelia's grip on the blankets tightened and she bit down hard on her lower lip to keep from filling the room with the sounds of her pleasure. Not only was Clint driving into her harder and harder, she was rocking back on her heels along with his rhythm so she could feel him pound into her with even more force. Eventually, Amelia lifted one leg and set her knee on the edge of the bed so she could lean forward and allow Clint to pump as deeply as possible.

Clint let her hair slip through his fingers and placed his hands once more upon her hips. He moved one hand along the thigh that was now resting on the edge of the bed. At the last second, he took hold of her there and pulled her toward him as he buried his cock deep inside of her.

Amelia arched her back and let out a breathy moan. When she felt Clint do the same thing again, she felt the heat inside of her grow until it threatened to boil over. She clenched her eyes shut and grabbed onto the bed with both hands as a powerful orgasm ripped through her body. When it passed, she felt unsteady on her feet and a little dizzy.

Seeing the way her knees were buckling, Clint pulled out of her and lifted her onto the bed. By the time she crawled onto the mattress, Amelia was feeling her strength return and motioned for Clint to lay down next to her.

The second Clint had stretched out on his back, Amelia

was on top of him. She straddled his cock and lowered herself onto it, taking in every inch with a smile that grew as she eased down lower. Once she had him all the way inside, her eyes were closed and she was leaning back to savor the moment.

Placing her hands upon her knees, Amelia started making little grinding motions with her hips. They started off slow, but built as she felt him growing harder and harder inside of her. When she began rocking back and forth, she let out a measured breath as another orgasm built up within her.

Clint's hands were on her legs. For the first couple minutes, he just lay back and enjoyed what Amelia was doing. Her slender body rose up over him. The more she put into her movements, the more her perky breasts swayed and bounced. Her pink little nipples were hard and erect, reminding Clint of tasty bits of candy. As much as he wanted to reach them, he didn't want to break Amelia's concentration. After all, she was doing a fine job on her own.

She was rocking faster now, riding his cock as her climax inched closer and closer. She barely seemed to notice Clint's hands moving up over her legs. When those hands made it to her inner thighs, she opened her eyes slightly. When Clint used his thumb to tease her clitoris while she impaled herself upon him, Amelia's eyes shot open and her lips curled into a surprised smile.

"Oh my God," she whispered.

Her eyes soon began to glaze over as Clint found the perfect rhythm in which to rub her. Soon, Amelia moved her hands up over the front of her own body until she cupped her breasts and began playing with her nipples as if she was having a private moment alone.

Clint didn't mind watching her quietly one bit.

In fact, the more excited she got, the better she moved on top of him. She didn't need her eyes to be open to move in perfect harmony with Clint. As he rubbed her clitoris faster, she would match his pace with her own hands and hips.

Soon, she was trembling and gasping for air as her muscles clenched in preparation for another climax. Amelia worked Clint up to those same heights until both of them were anxiously awaiting their release.

Amelia got there a second ahead of him and froze with her back arched and her head leaning in that same direction.

Clint pumped his hips up only once, which was enough to push both of them completely over the edge.

THIRTY-THREE

It was early the next morning when a small cart rattled down the street that cut Hendricks in two. The cart came to a stop and a man climbed down to walk silently up to the Copperhead Saloon. Although the Copperhead stayed open for all but two hours a night, the place was so empty that it didn't look open by any stretch.

The man stepped up to the bat-wing doors and peered over the top of them. He saw a few workers cleaning up the previous night's mess, a couple of drunks leaning against the bar, and a few card games still in progress.

It didn't take long for one of the workers to notice the man standing at the door. "Can I help you?" he asked.

Frank gazed in and reluctantly met the worker's eyes. "I'm looking for someone."

"If they're in here, you'd probably have better luck coming inside."

Since the worker could tell his banter was lost on the old man, he shifted to a more businesslike tone and said, "We're open for business, sir. You're welcome to come inside and look for whoever you want."

Frank pushed open the doors and walked in while letting out a breath as if he'd just stepped foot into the bowels

131

of a swamp. With a pinched expression on his face, he walked past the bar and toward the card games being played further inside the place.

One of the card tables was surrounded by well-dressed men with large piles of chips and cash in front of them. The middle of the table had an equally impressive treasure consisting of more chips, more cash, and even the spare piece of glittering jewelry. Frank turned away from that table without even being noticed by the players.

The next table wasn't carrying a fraction of the load of the first. In fact, this one was stacked mostly with pocket change and a few wadded bills. Frank walked past that one as well.

The next one caught the old man's interest immediately. Sitting there were a bunch of shabbily dressed men with varying degrees of stubble on their faces. The air around them smelled of dust, tobacco, and livestock. What caught Frank's eye most of all, however, was something else all those men had in common.

Every one of them was wearing a gun.

"Hey there, old timer," one of the gunmen said. "Looking to buy into a game?"

"No," Frank replied evenly.

"Then are you looking to buy us a round of drinks?"

Frank didn't even respond to that one.

"Because if it ain't one of those two things," the cowboy explained, "you'd best just keep on walking."

"I'm not here for either of those," Frank said. "I want to hire someone to kill a man."

The Bella Donna wasn't open for business, but there was still plenty going on behind its locked doors. To anyone who knew places like that as well as Mr. Cumberland did, it was common knowledge that all the real business happened behind tightly locked doors.

It took a bit of convincing, but the front doors were

eventually opened for a moment. That was just long enough to allow a few sloppy cowboys to barge in wearing beaming smiles on their faces. They were blocked from every room but one by hulking gunmen. Inside that last room, Mr. Cumberland was sitting eating freshly made eggs Benedict.

"You ain't gonna believe what just happened," Red said as he hurried over to Cumberland's table.

"You finally agreed to take a bath?" Cumberland asked. After taking a few loud sniffs of the air, he said, "No. That's obviously not it. Why don't you tell me?"

"You know that hired gun that was following around Jake McKean?"

"Yes."

"I just talked to a man who'll hand him over to us."

Cumberland's eyes widened a bit as he lifted a fork of runny eggs to his mouth. "Go on."

"He's some farmer that lives outside of town," Red said. "He came straight into the Copperhead, pretty as you please, walked over to our table, and asked if we'd kill a man for him."

"Why on earth would he come to you and ask for such a thing?"

"He says some old shopkeeper said that he could hire a gun there. Seems that someone's been wrangling his daughter and that didn't set too well with the old man one bit."

Gripping his knife a bit tighter, Cumberland asked, "This man is raping a child?"

"Nah, she's a pretty thing and plenty old enough. I guess her father's just the protective sort."

That caused Cumberland to ease up enough to dig back into his breakfast. "Protective doesn't quite seem to do him justice."

"Yeah, well, he's plenty pissed and wants this man dead. He says he's some gunman with a stab wound in his back. A wound that one of my boys put into a gunman not too long ago and not too far from here. The times match up and everything."

"That's still not a sure bet," Cumberland pointed out.

"Maybe not," Red said with a grin. "But he says this gunman brought a friend over to dinner just last night. The friend's name was Jake and he matched that skinny courier's description right down to the letter."

Chewing on his breakfast, Cumberland nodded slowly. "Did he, now?"

"He sure as hell did."

"And this old man wants you to kill this man for touching his daughter? Nothing more?"

"Sounds to me like he touched her quite a bit, but yeah. That's why he wants the son of a bitch dead."

"And he told you where to find this gunman?"

Red nodded. "He sure did. He even offered to keep him there long enough for us to get over there and pull the trigger whenever we pleased."

"Now this is good news," Cumberland said while setting his fork down and dabbing at his chin with a napkin. "All of this because of some recommendation from a store owner?"

Red shrugged and said, "I guess he thinks the Copperhead is a place where a bad sort spends their time."

"Imagine that. I suppose you'll be needing some more of my men to come along with you?"

This was the first time that Red's grin faltered in the slightest. "My crew has been thinning out a bit. I hope you got some boys that are better than the last ones you sent."

"Those were stand-ins," Cumberland assured him. "I've been saving the real players for the moment when they were truly needed."

"And that's now?" Red asked hopefully.

"Yes, that's now."

"Good to hear, sir."

"Maybe even better than you know." As Cumberland

said that, he nodded toward the door where one of the guards was leaning in.

"Someone's here to see you, Mr. Cumberland."

"Excellent. Show him in. As for you," he said to Red and the men who'd come in with him, "show yourselves out the back door. I don't think it would be good for my guest to see you here."

Although they were reluctant at first, Red and the other cowboys moved just as soon as the bulky guards started walking toward them. As soon as the cowboys were gone, Cumberland put on a smile and sipped his coffee.

"Hello there," he said to the new guest that was shown in. "Are you Jake McKean?"

"Yes, sir," Jake said as he pulled off his hat. "That'd be me."

THIRTY-FOUR

As much as Clint had wanted to go in with Jake for his meeting with the man from the company that scouted land for the railroad, he knew he wouldn't be allowed within sight of those documents. Men had a tendency to get real paranoid when it came to handling money. The men who already had a lot of money were already paranoid enough at the start.

So Clint waited around the corner where there were enough people milling about or walking by for him to blend into the scenery. The moment Jake had disappeared from sight, however, Clint had started to feel concern knotting the middle of his belly.

The fact that the Bella Donna was closed up tighter than the neckline of a spinster's dress didn't help matters either.

But there wasn't much of anything that Clint could do to help Jake or loosen the knot in his gut. For the moment, the only thing left for him to do was sit tight, nod to the folks who walked by, and wait.

After what felt like an entire change of the seasons, Clint saw the door to the Bella Donna open and Jake emerge as if he'd been spit out of the building. The skinny man took his sweet time in weaving through the growing traffic on the street and working his way over to the corner where Clint was waiting.

"I thought you were going to keep out of sight," Jake said.

"And I thought you were only going to be gone for a few minutes," Clint shot back.

Jake grinned and cocked his head a bit. "I knew you were starting to come around. You always act like we're butting heads, but I knew we'd be friends soon enough."

"Just tell me what happened in there."

"It went off just fine. Granted, this wasn't the spot where I was supposed to meet him, but that's only because of all the shooting that's been going on around here. Even though I know the reason behind it, I can't say as I blame him for being skittish."

"So he's the one you were supposed to meet up with?" Clint asked.

"Sure," Jake replied. "I've never met up with the same man twice, but they all start to look the same after a while. They're all dressed like dandies and surrounded with men who look like they'd snap you in half rather than look at you."

"Did anything seem out of place?"

"Out of place?"

"Jesus Christ, don't you remember anything we talked about before you went in there?"

Jake nodded quickly and replied, "Sure I do, but everything was just like it should be."

"Did he hand over the documents he was supposed to give you?"

"He sure did," Jake said as he patted his jacket. Just to emphasize his point, he opened his jacket enough for Clint to see the papers that were folded and stuffed into the inside pocket. "See?"

"So he just handed them over. What did you do to fill up the rest of the time you were in there?"

"He offered me a drink, which I took. It's not every day that I get to have a glass of imported whiskey. None of the other fellas I've met up with were so generous."

"And that's all?"

"Actually, there was something else that never happened before."

Pulling in a breath, Clint had to force himself not to wrap his hands around Jake's throat and squeeze. "What else, Jake?" Clint asked in a measured tone.

"He asked me about the other papers I've been carrying."

"You mean the documents?"

Jake nodded.

"The same documents that men have been trying to kill you to get?"

Jake nodded again.

"If none of the others asked to see those documents," Clint said, "don't you think that qualifies as something out of the ordinary?"

Jake actually had to stop and think that over for a moment before his eyes widened and he started to nod. "You know, that does fit into that category. Maybe it's the whiskey, but I just didn't think too much about it."

"What did he say regarding those papers?" Clint asked.

"He asked to see them all. He said he needed to check their authenticity. When I told him I didn't bring them, he asked where they were."

Clint lifted his hand to his face so he could rub the throbbing pain that had just started to crop up at his temples. "Did you tell him where they were?"

"No. That was one of the specific instructions I got at the beginning of this. Nobody else was supposed to see more than one set of them papers other than the men in Sacramento. That's how they keep it so nobody knows much more than anyone else."

Ignoring the condescending tone in Jake's voice, Clint asked, "What's this man's name?"

"Mr. Cumberland. I didn't catch a first name."

"And you're certain he works for the right people?"

"Yes . . . well . . . I think so. He did give me this." Saying that, Jake reached into his jacket and removed the folded papers from the inner pocket. Flipping them over, he tapped a wax seal with his finger. "It's sealed up like all the others. That's how I know they're authentic. I remember that as well."

"More specific instructions, huh?"

Jake nodded, tapped his forehead, and slipped the papers back into his pocket. "Now that I think about it, there's no way he could be an imposter. Maybe we're being suspicious for no good reason."

"Or," Clint said, "maybe this Mr. Cumberland is the genuine article, but wants to see more than his portion of that report. Being the last man on your route would mean he would just need to get a hold of you in order to put that entire document together."

"Oh. I never thought about that."

THIRTY-FIVE

"What, exactly, did you say when he asked you about the rest of the documents?"

"I said they were in safe keeping and being watched by a trusted partner," Jake answered proudly.

Clint's eyes were now focused upon the line of men who'd walked out of the Bella Donna and were headed straight for them. "And did you happen to mention that your partner was waiting around the corner?"

With his back still to the Bella Donna, Jake winked and gave Clint a grin. "Not even a hint. Specific instructions, after all."

"Yeah. Something tells me that he's not too worried about those instructions."

By now, Jake could see that Clint's attention was being diverted by something behind him. He turned around and got a look at the men who had come from the Bella Donna. Even though he hadn't seen them leave the place, he recognized those bulky monsters without any trouble whatsoever.

"What are they doing out here?" Jake asked incredulously.

"My guess is they want to have a word with you. I might

expect them to bring up those papers you're carrying as well."

"But they know I don't have the rest. I told them someone else was watching over them."

"Then, maybe your Mr. Cumberland figures he knows where to find your partner and get those documents. Either way, we've got our hands full right about now."

"These men aren't like those others," Jake sputtered as he stood next to Clint and faced the oncoming hulks. "They're killers. I could see it in their eyes."

"No need to tell me that. I could see it all the way from here."

"So, what do we do?"

"Whatever we have to," Clint replied. "You going to be all right?"

"I guess."

"Then just keep your head on your shoulders and don't mention that I'm your partner. If things get rough, just follow my lead."

"Will you give me a signal?"

"Believe me," Clint said, "I won't have to."

Since the men from the Bella Donna were taking their sweet time in approaching them, Clint and Jake were as ready as they could be by the time they got there.

"Can I help you gentlemen?" Clint asked politely.

The men were dressed in dark suits that were almost tailored well enough to completely hide the guns under their arms. There were three of them in all, but they had enough combined muscle to form at least another man or two.

The man in the middle of the group stood nearly a foot taller than Clint. Like the other two, this one had wide shoulders and a neck that was just as thick as the rest of his head. When he got a close look at him, Clint wondered how many times he'd have to hit the big man before he made a dent or was even noticed.

"Who are you?" the big man asked in a smooth, confident voice.

"I was just standing here talking to Jake. Did I do something wrong?"

The eyes of all three of those giants looked Clint up and down with such intensity that Clint felt as if he was physically being searched. After such close scrutiny, Clint still couldn't get much of a read on whether or not the men were about to take him apart.

"Are you a friend of Jake's?" the big man in the middle asked.

Clint chuckled and replied, "Not if it's going to get me in trouble."

There wasn't even a fraction of a smile between all three of the giants. The one in the middle glanced down at the Colt on Clint's hip and then looked over to Jake.

"Mr. Cumberland wants to see those documents."

Jake tried to follow Clint's example, but he simply couldn't stay as calm. "I . . . uh . . . you mean the ones he gave me? Why . . . um . . . is there a problem?"

"No. There's not a problem. He just needs to see them. By that, I mean the ones he gave you as well as any others you have on you."

"I told him that I didn't have the rest on me."

"Mr. Cumberland wants us to double check on that." Without another word, all three of the giants surged forward. One of them reached out to grab hold of Jake's arms. The one in the middle nearly ripped Jake's chest off as he took the documents from his inner jacket pocket and the third man stepped forward to get between Clint and the rest like some kind of living wall.

"I can't let you take that," Jake said with a speed that even seemed to surprise himself.

The giant who'd taken the documents from Jake looked surprised as well. Actually, he looked part surprised and part amused. "You can't let me take . . . this?" As he said that, the giant finished what he was doing and wound up with the documents clutched between his beefy fingers. "I suppose you're going to tell me next that you won't be able to help me get the rest of those papers?"

When he said that last part, the giant's voice made it sound more like a dare than a question.

"I . . . ahh . . . really can't do that," Jake squeaked.

Clint had to give Jake some credit right about now. Considering the menace written all over the faces of those three monsters, Jake was holding his own fairly well. Of course, there was always the possibility that the man simply didn't know how hot the water was getting.

The man standing between Clint and the others took one step back and squared his shoulders while lowering his hand and flicking open his jacket. Both of the others made similar movements, which freed them up to draw their guns that much easier.

"We can always take those papers from you," the first giant said. "Because we already know where the rest are at."

"No need for threats," Jake said with a shaky smile. "We don't want anyone to get hurt."

The giant grinned and replied, "Oh, it's too late to avoid that."

THIRTY-SIX

Seeing the look in those big men's eyes, Clint knew there was no way to get away from that spot without a fight. The blood had already been spilled in those guards' minds. The only question that remained was how much would stain the street.

"Last chance," the giant said.

Whether it was out of courage or from the knowledge that there wasn't really any other choice, Jake shook his head and started moving away from the big man in front of him.

"No," Jake said. "You're just going to shoot me anyway."

"We've got no reason to do that after we get those documents. Especially out here, in the middle of the street with everybody watching." To make his point, the giant took a look around and added, "Not a very private place for a murder."

Jake surprised Clint yet again by glancing over to him and smiling with relief. "He's right."

"Aw, hell," Clint grunted as he saw the giant closest to Jake reach for the gun holstered under his arm.

For a man of his size, the giant was a surprisingly quick draw. His hand flickered beneath his jacket and when it reappeared, it was wrapped around a Navy-model Colt that was polished to an immaculate shine.

Clint's first impulse was to draw and fire his own Colt, but that would still leave Jake with a fresh bullet hole somewhere in his body. At that range, there was no way for the giant to miss. For that reason, Clint snapped his hand out toward Jake rather than his holster, so he could toss the skinny man out of the line of fire.

The giant's gun roared and sent a plume of smoke into the air. The bullet hissed dangerously close to Jake's body, but Clint's efforts had kept him from catching even a taste of lead. Jake was thrown with such force that he flopped to the ground and knocked the side of his head against the nearby boardwalk.

Even though Clint had managed to save Jake from that first shot, there were plenty more on their way. That was mainly due to the fact that the other two hulking men had now had enough time to draw their own guns.

Clint paused for a second, which seemed like an eternity. The only reason he waited at all was so the bigger men could get one more chance to think twice before following through. Either the monsters were too confident or too stupid to ease up because all three of them lifted their guns and took aim.

Clint watched everything as if the events were happening to someone else. In his eyes, things spooled out slowly, allowing him to feel the blood racing through his veins and the hammering of his heart in his chest.

Even as he reached for the Colt at his side, Clint worried that he would be shot long before his finger touched the trigger. Those kinds of thoughts always rushed through a man's head at the start of a fight. And, just like in every other fight, Clint shoved those thoughts to one side and focused on what needed to be done if he was going to see another day above ground.

In a smooth, practiced motion, Clint lifted the Colt from

its holster and pointed it at the man who had his sights on him. While dropping to one knee, Clint brought up the gun and fired. Thunder filled his ears from not only his own gun, but from the gun that had been fired at him.

Lead hissed through the air like an angry wasp, but was a few inches over Clint's head.

The man who'd fired at Clint twitched back as blood sprayed from his ribs. His eyes flashed with the pain of hot lead tearing through his flesh, but the man still kept his gun pointed in Clint's direction.

Clint wasn't paying much attention to that, however. Knowing that the bigger man meant to kill him, he intended on putting his target down no matter how long it took.

The moment he felt his knee touch against the ground, Clint steadied himself and adjusted his aim. He squeezed his trigger once more, this time, sending a round through the bigger man's right eye and out the back of his skull.

Like a puppet whose strings had been cut, the giant's arms dropped to his sides and his knees wobbled beneath him. His finger tensed around his trigger thanks to his dying reflex and sent a bullet into the dirt. His body fell over and hit the ground while the battle raged on without him.

More shots cracked through the air, only half of which were being fired at Clint. Jake was doing a hell of a job staying alive, but that was mainly because he was so awkward while trying to run away that it was impossible to guess where to aim.

Jake had managed to draw his gun and was firing shots in the general direction of the other men. Other than that, he was lucky to be alive.

One of the two remaining monsters fired a shot at Clint while filling his other hand with a second gun from under his jacket. Clint took a quick shot at him, but only managed to graze the giant's hip. It was a wound that would be felt a while later, once the heat of battle had died down. For the moment, however, Clint knew he was still in trouble.

As soon as the bigger man had both guns in hand, he pulled both triggers and sent a hailstorm of lead in Clint's direction. Rather than return fire, Clint pushed off with both legs and threw himself toward a nearby watering trough. He felt something dig into his stomach and ribs, but that was only the top of the trough as he jumped over it. The instant his legs hit the ground, Clint pressed his back against the trough and hoped for the best.

With the combination of ringing in his ears and the drumming of his own pulse echoing through his head, Clint heard nothing but his own breaths and something knocking against wood. That knocking was the passage of bullets through the trough as hole after hole was punched through it.

Since he was still breathing and able to move, Clint twisted around to take a few shots of his own. He caught sight of the two-gun shooter and immediately pulled his trigger. The first round from the Colt sailed well out of range, but the second drew a bit closer. Both of the other man's guns were still blasting away, however, which meant Clint had no other choice but to keep blasting back.

Forcing himself to take a breath, Clint eased off on his trigger and got his target more clearly in his sights. He then sighted down the Colt's barrel, clenched his teeth through a sudden pain that had started blazing through his side, and fired.

That shot brought the hailstorm to a stop as the big two-gun shooter was rocked back by a hit to the chest. Another shot came soon after and only widened the hole through his torso. After both bullets were through with him, most of the big man's heart was spilling down his back. From there, all the two-gun shooter could do was fall.

Even though Clint knew the Colt was empty, the air around him was still full of lead. A few rounds chipped away at his portion of the trough, but most of the action was taking place a few feet to Clint's side. Keeping his back pressed tightly against the trough, Clint flipped open the Colt's cylinder and started reloading.

THIRTY-SEVEN

Once he'd been shoved to the ground, Jake had done his best to keep his wits about him and stay alive. Considering everything that had happened, he was pretty impressed that he was still managing to keep from filling a casket just yet.

Somehow, he'd managed to get his gun in his hand and return fire. What amazed him even more was that he'd gotten himself behind the same bit of cover that Clint had found. Of course, the only problem was that Jake was still only one wrong move away from becoming just another body in the dirt.

As the seconds ticked by and dying felt like more and more of a real possibility, Jake couldn't even recall what was so important to have sparked the fight in the first place. Luckily for him, he never got the chance to do much thinking at all.

Jake could practically feel every one of the last giant's steps thumping off the ground. Those impacts rattled all the way up through his body like cannonballs dropping from the sky. One quick glance told him that the bigger man only needed to take a few more steps before he had a clear shot at the back of Jake's head.

Rather than sit still for that to happen, Jake twisted around and pointed his gun at the approaching giant.

He'd never been much of a shot, but Jake's ability to think on his feet and move quick as the tip of a snake's tongue had seen him through the couple of bad situations he'd been in. This time, however, there were no more places to hide and no chance of running away.

Jake needed to fight.

Fight or die.

There couldn't be more than two shots left in his pistol. As he rolled away from the trough, Jake saw one of the giant's boots land on the ground in front of him. He didn't wait one more second before shooting at the only target in his sight.

Jake pointed his gun at that boot and pulled his trigger until the hammer was slapping against empty brass.

The giant had taken a shot before he felt something burn through his right shin. That was followed by something else burning through his right foot. After that, his momentum forced him to step down upon that same side, which made his entire body explode with a pain that all but consumed him.

Jake had already heard the empty clanking from his gun enough to know it was empty. Even so, he grinned when he saw the bigger man grit his teeth and start to topple over thanks to the gunshots that had torn through his right leg and foot.

Jake's smile lasted right up until he saw the giant shift his weight over to his left side, steady himself, and look for his target with a fresh fire in his eyes.

Having already gotten to his feet a moment ago, Jake found himself in the open now that the bigger gunman had stopped his own fall. He thought about throwing his gun at the giant, but that seemed to make as much sense as trying to chop down a tree with a pocketknife.

The only option left for Jake was to reload and fire again.

Given the time he had left, Jake figured he might be able to get his hands on a single bullet before being shot clean out of his boots.

Suddenly, Jake heard another series of shots. They weren't coming from the giant's gun, however. Instead, like an answer to his prayers, they came at the giant and hit the bigger man square in the chest.

Standing up from behind the trough, Clint fired from the hip and unleashed the rounds he'd just loaded into his Colt. The first shot hadn't done much, but every one after that was right on target. What worried him was the fact that the shots still didn't seem to be doing much more than bouncing off the bigger man's hide.

Even as he took round after round, the giant didn't do more than flinch. His eyes flickered shut and then popped back open until all but the last shot in Clint's gun were fired. Even as the roar of those shots drifted away and the smoke rolled between them, all three men simply stood where they were and waited for the next shoe to drop.

Jake was still smiling, but was starting to back away.

The giant was teetering back on his left leg, which supported his weight, thanks to some impossible feat of balance.

Clint straightened up from his defensive crouch and sighted along the barrel of his Colt. He knew there was only one shot left in his gun. Normally, he would figure that last shot would cap off the other man nicely. After seeing the giant take bullet after bullet like an angry grizzly, his thoughts on that matter were starting to change.

Now, Clint thought that firing one more shot would just be a waste of time and ammunition.

The giant's lips curled back to reveal a large set of clenched teeth. He glared at Clint through squinted eyes and started to lift his gun hand to take a shot. Then, all of the wounds he'd gotten seemed to catch up to him in a rush.

His head drooped forward and his shoulders became hunched.

With one last effort, the big man stumbled toward Clint. That effort caused him to put his weight upon his right leg, which was the last mistake he would ever make. Letting out a pained groan, the big man's leg gave way and he fell straight to the ground. He landed in a heap, let out a breath, and gave up the ghost.

Reluctantly, Jake stepped forward and watched the body of that fallen giant.

Clint quickly reloaded the Colt and moved forward as well. Even before he took more than two steps, Clint knew the big man was dead. Just to be certain, he snapped the Colt shut and kept it in his hand while looking to make sure there weren't any more gunmen headed his way.

Apart from plenty of gaping witnesses to the fight, Jake was the only one left in Clint's sight who was still drawing breath.

"Nice shooting," Clint said as relief finally allowed him to let out the breath he'd been holding.

Jake wiped away the sweat rolling from his forehead and said, "Damn. I wonder if that boy's name was Goliath?"

"Don't get too proud of yourself, David," Clint said. "This isn't over yet."

THIRTY-EIGHT

The cart rattled up to the Learner house and came to a stop. Even before Amelia could step down from the battered vehicle, her father was glaring at her through the front window. By the time both her feet were on the ground, she heard the front door fly open and Frank stomp outside.

"Where's that friend of yours?" the old man asked.

"You mean Clint?"

"Yeah."

"He's gone."

"He was supposed to be gone yesterday, but he still came back around for dinner. Where'd he go?"

Amelia's brow furrowed as she fixed her father with a stern look. "I may put up with a lot from you, but that doesn't mean I'll let you talk to me like I'm some disobedient child. In case you haven't noticed, I'm a grown—"

"Where've you been, anyway?" Frank interrupted.

Amelia's hands were balled up on her hips and she was obviously ready for a fight. Since her opponent seemed to have already moved on to better things, she let out an aggravated breath and turned back around to the cart. "I was over at Melissa's," she said while taking a bundle that had been sitting on the footboard of the cart.

"Melissa's? What the hell for?"

"She fixed this dress of mine," Amelia said while quickly flaring the skirt she was wearing. "Isn't it nice? She also mended some of those old shirts you refuse to throw away. They're right here."

"Guess that explains why you haven't heard the commotion from in town."

"Commotion?" Amelia asked as the color drained from her face. "What are you talking about? What sort of commotion?"

"There's been shooting. Your brother ran off so he could hear it better."

"Oh my God."

"My guess is that your friend Clint Adams is in the middle of whatever it is that's happening. I told you he was trouble. I told you to let him lay in the mud until a doctor could collect him and drag him into town where men like him belong."

Amelia was feeling her balance start to slip away, so she leaned against the cart. "Be quiet," she said. "Just let me catch my breath."

But rather than respond to the way his daughter had paled and was now trying to keep from falling over, Frank took the offensive. He leaned forward and raised his voice until it was something close to a snarl. "I told you not to bother with him, but you wouldn't listen! I told you men like him won't do nothin' but hurt you and you still take that son of a bitch into your bed!"

When she heard that, Amelia found the strength not only to stand on her own, but to slap her father across his face. The impact of her hand against his cheek was louder than the gunshots that had made it to the Learner's place like distant thunder. It was also loud enough to momentarily shut Frank's mouth.

Judging by the look on Amelia's face, she was just as stunned by what she'd done as her father was.

"There," she said. "Maybe now you'll stop talking and hear me out for a change."

Frank raised a hand to his face and touched his cheek as if he expected the skin to be split open. After lowering his hand, he kept his eyes on his daughter and his mouth closed.

"First of all," Amelia said, "the only reason I'm still living here is because you made me promise to stay after Mother died. Even then, I wasn't going to stay until you swore to let me carry on with my own life and be treated like the grown woman I am."

"I never wanted to—"

She cut Frank off with nothing more than a swiftly raised finger.

"Don't try to talk nice now," she said. "And don't try to act like you were just protecting me."

"But I was." Sweeping his hand toward Hendricks, Frank added, "I was protecting you from that. Protecting you from them that comes from there because there's men in towns like that who want nothing more than to take what they want from you and move on. Just like that bastard that's been taking advantage of you!"

"What did you say to me?"

"You heard what I said. I ain't stupid. I know that you and him were alone together."

"So what?" Amelia snapped. "Whatever you and the rest of those coots you call friends may think, women don't just sit around pining for their knight in shining armor to come calling. We may share some time with a man and we may even share our beds with some, but we still don't do half the carousing that you men do when you're in the mood."

Frank sputtered as if he was trying to spit out a string of words before he even knew what he wanted to say. Before he thought of anything, his daughter came up with plenty more that she wanted to say.

"I help pay for this land," she said. "I help take care of it. I help care for the house and I help with Dave. I can do whatever the hell I want to do in my own home so long as it doesn't hurt anyone. If you even think I've done anything to cause one bit of harm, I swear to God I'll never talk to you again."

"You didn't hurt anyone," Frank said quietly. "I just wanted to make certain that nobody hurt you."

"Do I look hurt to you?"

He looked her up and down before reluctantly shaking his head. "No, but that doesn't—"

"And do you think I've hurt anyone else?"

"No!"

"Then mind your own damn business and keep your nose out of mine! I love you, but if I've got to yell to get through to you, then so be it. I can take care of myself. Lord knows I've taken care of you and Dave for long enough to prove that for damn sure."

Frank was still looking at his daughter in disbelief. For what seemed like the hundredth time, he lifted a hand to his face and rubbed the spot that was already beginning to turn red. "I . . . can't believe you hit me."

Rolling her eyes, Amelia rubbed her father's face and said, "I've seen you get worse than that by running into a door."

"I know, but . . . you hit me!"

"And I'd do it again if that's what it takes to get through that damn head of yours. Is this business finished?"

"I . . . I guess."

"What about that shooting?" Amelia asked as she turned to look at the town. "Do you know who's doing it?"

"I . . . don't think so."

"I hope Clint isn't in any trouble." As she said that, Amelia was turning around to look for Dave. Her eyes just happened to find her father again and stayed there when she saw the older man's expression.

"What is it?" she asked. "What aren't you telling me?"

"Just that . . . maybe . . . this business with Clint may not be over."

"What do you mean?" When she didn't get an answer right away, Amelia rushed forward and grabbed her father by the shoulders. "What do you mean?" she asked while shaking him.

"I thought he was hurting you," Frank said, although his voice and eyes made it clear that even he didn't believe that. "I thought he was taking advantage of you."

"Oh my God, Papa. What did you do?"

THIRTY-NINE

There was usually always someone coming or going from Hendricks. The town wasn't the biggest, but it was large enough to have a steady trickle of riders moving through it. But even that trickle had something of a pattern to it. At least, it did for anyone who watched it long enough. And since they'd lived outside of that town for their entire lives, the Learners had no trouble at all spotting the riders that didn't fit within the pattern.

They rode in a straight line at first. As soon as they were outside the town's limits, they straightened out into a row and headed directly for the homestead set up on the outskirts.

Dave was the first one to spot them and had come running back to the house to report what he'd seen. As soon as Frank and Amelia laid eyes on those riders, they knew they weren't just more travelers heading out of Hendricks.

"Looks like somebody's coming," Dave said excitedly.

"That's right," Amelia muttered. "It sure does."

A few moments earlier, Frank told his daughter about going to the Copperhead and asking around for some men to do a dirty job for him. As she'd listened, Amelia had felt sick to her stomach. She'd fought that down, however, and kept from crying. There wasn't enough time for tears.

At least, not yet.

The riders picked up speed and headed toward the house like a volley of arrows. The closer they got, the faster they came. Finally, after what felt like only a few heartbeats later, they were thundering over the fences that Frank had put up, which had been enough to keep their few head of livestock from escaping.

Those fences weren't even close to keeping Red and his gunmen out.

"What's going on, Pa?" Dave asked as he followed behind his father and sister. "Who are those men?"

Frank was running to the house where his hunting rifle was stored while Amelia prepared their other horse for a quick getaway.

"They're the ones that were after Clint," Amelia said before Frank could get out a single word.

"But Clint ain't here," Dave said. "They can look all they want and they won't find him."

Amelia stopped in the middle of pulling open the barn doors. The horse inside was anxiously stomping on the floor as if it knew how close it was to a good, hard run. But Amelia wasn't about to let it out just yet. In fact, she closed it and turned around to face her brother.

"Those men are coming because they were hired to kill Clint and told that Clint was here," Amelia said to herself more than to her brother.

But Dave didn't pick up on that difference one bit. His eyes turned wide as saucers and his mouth gaped open. "They're coming to kill Clint? You know that for sure?"

She nodded absently, but her eyes were already jumping ahead to the house. "They were told to come get him, but there were already plenty of shots fired in town."

Dave nodded furiously at that. "There sure were. I heard 'em!"

"It would be too much of a coincidence for there to be a shooting in town at the same time as those men riding out here and for them not to be connected."

"Huh?"

Amelia walked straight to her brother and spoke as if she was about to win a debate with the younger boy. "Clint's in town at the same time there's all this trouble, which means he's got to be wrapped up in that shooting somehow. But if those men are still coming here, that means they must not be after Clint."

"Maybe they want to be where he was," Dave offered.

"Or maybe they're after something else."

The moment she said that, Amelia felt the bottom fall out of her stomach. Something terrible had leapt into her head and almost escaped out of her mouth.

What if those men weren't after Clint at all?

What if they were after Jake and thought he was still hiding somewhere on the Learners' property?

Or what if her father was right and those men were coming to do their worst to her and her family? She couldn't think of a reason why someone would do that, but all those years of suspiciously eyeing that town reared up and clenched tightly around Amelia's throat.

She grabbed hold of her brother and spun him around so she could look directly into his eyes.

"Do you have somewhere to hide?" she asked.

"Yeah, but it ain't big enough for nobody else."

"It doesn't matter. Just go and hide there."

"But why—"

"Run!"

FORTY

The riders got to the Learner place and spread out so they could work their way through it in one pass. Their horses were still breathing heavy from the hard ride from town, which made their hooves slam against the dirt especially hard as they walked. Compared to the animals themselves, the men on their backs might as well have been statues.

Those men already had their guns drawn and were searching for a target. Whenever they heard the slightest sound, they pointed their guns in that direction and waited to see if anything would move. After they met up at the other side of the property, they turned back around and faced the small group of old buildings.

"You men split up that way," Red said as he waved to the left. "You men head off that way," he said while waving to the right. To the men that remained, he said, "The rest of you come with me."

"What are we looking for?" one of the new additions to Red's crew asked.

"Either Jake or that gunman that was with him. If they ain't back here yet, then anything walking on two legs will do. Just be sure to keep whoever you find alive. I've got some questions I need to ask."

161

Nodding, the men with Red followed the cowboy straight down the middle of the path that led all the way back to town. The Learners' house and barn were both facing that path and the animal pens were off to the side.

While Red and his group moved past the fronts of those buildings, the other two groups of men circled around the backs on both sides of the path. As a soft wind blew, the horses worked their way slowly through the Learner homestead.

The only sounds to be heard were the breathing of the horses, the crunch of hooves against dirt, and the occasional creak of a rusty hinge.

Red had just gone past the front of the house when he saw one of the men in the other group signal to him from behind it. Leaning forward, Red locked eyes with the man and waited.

Rather than break the silence, the man at the back of the house tapped his ear and then pointed toward the house itself. Red nodded and then motioned for the other man to go back where he'd come from.

"He heard something inside," Red said to one of the men who was closer to him.

"You want me to get the others?"

"Nah. Harry knows what to do on his own. Let's clear out this house and see if they're all in one place to make it easier on us."

Red and his men swung down from their saddles and approached the front of the house. Just as they had when they got onto the property, the men spread out to form a row with their guns pointed straight ahead.

Standing to the left of the front door, Red nodded to the man in front of the door and stood aside while he kicked it off its hinges. As soon as the other cowboy's boot had slammed into the door, there was another sound that easily drowned out the noise of the kick.

The roar of a shotgun was distinctive enough to get all

the men in front of the house to duck and back away from the door. All the men but one, that is, since the man who'd kicked the door down had caught the brunt of that shotgun blast in his chest. His body flew a few feet straight back and landed in a lifeless heap.

The man to the right of the door was able to peek in through a window. He did so very carefully, but soon jumped to his feet and turned toward Red. "It's an old man. He's reloading!"

Red straightened up as well and charged in through the front door. Even though he was fairly certain he could take an old man brandishing an empty gun, he still allowed the other cowboy to lead the charge into the house.

"Son of a bitch," Frank muttered as he slapped a fresh load of buckshot into the breach and closed up his shotgun. The moment he felt the barrel snap into place, he pulled both triggers.

Although it wasn't as clean a shot as the first one, the blast widened out enough to catch a good piece of the next man to run through Frank's door. The buckshot shredded away the cowboy's jacket, shirt, and several layers of skin. A bloody mist was thrown into the air for good measure as the cowboy was spun off his feet and thrown against a wall.

Red saw his partner tossed aside as if he'd been swatted like a fly. Seeing that caused Red's finger to tighten reflexively around his trigger. His pistol bucked in his hand several times as he pulled his trigger again and again. All the while, Red gritted his teeth and ran for the first cover he could find, which happened to be an old chair not far from the door.

Once he was behind the chair, Red was still pulling his trigger. By now, the hammer was snapping down upon spent rounds with a loud metallic click. That clicking sound shook Red out of his daze so he could see that he was still alive and hiding behind a piece of ratty furniture.

Just then, the back door to the house was kicked in and

heavy steps pounded against the floor. Red peeked out from behind the chair and saw one group of his men filing into the front room. Doing his best to cover the panicked expression that had been on his face, Red stood up and stepped out from behind the chair.

"Jesus Christ," one of the cowboys said as he got a look at the two bodies near the front door.

"Some old man gunned these boys down," Red said. His eyes darted about the room, but he couldn't see anyone besides the other gunmen. "He must have gotten away."

"Looks like he was hit, though," one of the gunmen said as he squatted down to get a look at a fresh spatter of blood on the floor. "This leads upstairs."

Red's hand was shaking as he reloaded his pistol. "I'll go up there."

These gunmen had only recently been introduced to Red by Mr. Cumberland. Until now, they'd been content to take orders and go where Red pointed. Now that shots had been fired and blood had been spilled, they carried themselves in a different way.

Their eyes were more like those found in a wolf. They were predator's eyes and they marked the men as real killers.

"No," one of the gunmen snarled. "We'll get him."

Red wasn't about to get in their way.

FORTY-ONE

Amelia had lived in that house since she was two years old. Some of her earliest memories were the smell of fresh timber as she walked down the hall and the feel of the new boards under her little bare feet. She knew every inch of that house as well as every inch around and below it.

In fact, thanks to a game she'd used to play with her brother, she knew the area beneath that house especially well.

The root cellar was all but hidden and the doors leading down into it were so dirty that they practically blended in with the earth. But that cellar was too easy a spot for children to use for games of hide-and-go-seek. To win those games, Amelia had had to find a spot that was even better than the cellar.

A spot so good that nobody knew where it was.

A spot she could get to in a hurry without being seen.

A spot much like the space beneath the side of the house directly below the kitchen.

As a child, Amelia had hidden in that place and giggled into her hand while Dave had tried in vain to find her. She could hear his angry steps as he stomped around outside and cursed her name when he thought nobody else could hear him.

She'd huddled in that place and smelled her mother's cooking as she fixed supper and shouted out through the window for the children to come inside. She'd giggled then, too, thinking that even her parents were fooled.

Over the years, she'd gone from huddling to crawling just to get into that spot. Now, she was forced to lay flat on her stomach and slither into the trusty spot like a snake. As the riders had gotten closer, she'd gotten wedged halfway in with her feet hanging outside.

The sight was probably hilarious, but at the time she could think of nothing but feeling rough hands wrap around her ankles and haul her out. From there, her mind went through all sorts of hell, picturing what would be done to her next.

But those hands hadn't found her either.

She was able to tear free of the nail that had snagged her dress and pull herself the rest of the way inside. Although she wasn't able to move much once she was in, Amelia was able to again feel the safety that came from being stashed away from the rest of the world.

Curled up in a ball, she tried not to breathe in too deeply because that would only force out the sneeze that was perched at the back of her throat. Instead, she took quick gasps of air and held her breath when she got too close to making a noise that would give her away.

Apart from feeling eight sizes too small, the space felt much like it had when she'd first discovered it. That first time, it had been a dark, dirty, scary place where monsters lived. The more she ran into it, the brighter the place became, and the more her own, until she felt just as comfortable there as she did in her own bed.

Those days were long gone, however. Now, she felt dirty, cramped, and terrified. There might not have been any monsters in that space beneath the kitchen, but there sure were plenty of monsters in the house above her.

She knew there were at least three men in the house at first. Amelia could hear them talking and, after Frank's gun had gone off a few times, she could hear them hitting the floor with heavy thumps. But now that the others had come inside, there was no way for her to tell how many were stomping through her house.

To make matters worse, these new men walked more like cats than the first batch. Amelia could hear them whispering at first before they went almost completely silent. From what she could tell, the men had gone upstairs after her father.

Frank was definitely already upstairs. She recognized his footsteps just as easily as she could recognize his voice. Even though she knew he could handle himself, Amelia feared for her father's safety. He'd protected the house from countless robbers as well as a few killers, but he hadn't taken on the likes of these quiet men.

As she thought about her father being cornered all alone upstairs in the house where she'd grown up, Amelia couldn't stay put in hiding. It was her house as well and she couldn't simply hide beneath it while armed men stomped around wherever they pleased. That seemed especially out of place considering the argument she'd had with her father not too long ago.

After claiming to be a competent adult, Amelia felt truly idiotic running and hiding under the porch at the first sign of trouble. She lay in the dirt and closed her eyes, wondering just what the hell she could do that would be of any help. Even if she crawled out and snuck up on those men, she didn't know what to do next.

Kick them?

Scream at them?

Each choice seemed more ridiculous than the one before it, until her elbow brushed against something that had previously been covered with layers of dusty grit. It took quite a bit of shifting and squirming to reach the object, but Amelia finally shifted onto her side and felt around for the object that had caught her attention.

The second her fingers drifted over the cold steel, she knew that her first instinct had been right all along. She felt up along the steel until her hand brushed over a wooden grip and a trigger guard.

She smiled so widely that it practically lit up the dark space. Even though she couldn't see much of anything, she knew enough to keep the gun pointed away from her as she got it into her hands and opened the cylinder.

Dumping out the bullets allowed Amelia to feel the lead tips on half of them. The other half must have been fired some time ago, but there was no way for her to know how long. The fact of the matter was that she couldn't even see the gun in her hand. Just feeling the heavy pistol against her palm was more than enough to make her feel better.

She didn't even mind that her secret hiding space had been discovered somewhere along the way by the very person she'd originally been hiding from. Amelia pressed the gun to her face and nearly cried with relief.

"Thank you, Dave," she whispered.

FORTY-TWO

Harry led the third group of gunmen around the back of the barn. When he'd heard the shots coming from the house, his first impulse was to run and see if Red needed any help. He was stopped by a firm grip upon his shoulder, which kept him rooted to the spot.

"Where do you think you're going?" one of Cumberland's gunmen asked.

"Didn't you hear that?" Harry asked. "Those were gunshots!"

"And most of the men we brought with us are already there. Isn't there more than one person around here we're supposed to round up?"

"Well, yeah."

"Then we'll stay here. For all we know, those shots could be a distraction."

"Red might be hurt."

Suddenly, the gun in the other man's hand shifted to point directly at Harry. "And you'll be hurt next if you don't shut the hell up and do what I say."

Harry looked around at the other men. Until this very moment, he thought that he and Red were the ones leading this raid on the Learner place. Now that he saw the intensity in the other men's eyes, Harry had no doubt that he was the one meant to follow. He also was certain that Red wouldn't have any more luck trying to lead the men with him.

Rather than try to swim upstream, Harry nodded and motioned for the others to go on ahead.

"Those papers must be stashed somewhere around here," the lead gunman said.

Harry stuck his nose into the barn and took a quick peek. "How do we know that for sure?"

"Because that's what Mr. Cumberland said. That's all I need to know."

"Is it?"

"If they were on that courier, we would have been signaled back by now. Besides, that skinny asshole is like a rat. If he spends enough time nesting in one spot, he's bound to leave something behind."

"Yeah," Harry grunted. "Like a whole pile of scat."

None of the other men seemed to think that was as funny as Harry himself did. Harry's laughter died off quickly after he received a few stern glares.

"You're right. We should keep quiet."

Shifting his eyes from Harry as if he'd suddenly decided the cowboy didn't exist, the gunman who'd taken the lead of that group pushed open the side door to the barn. "That courier wasn't carrying those papers on him. And they weren't on his horse either."

"How do you know?" Harry asked.

"We just do. That means they must be here, since this is the last place Jake spent any time. He was under strict orders to hide those papers whenever he could so they didn't have to be in the open for much time at a stretch."

Harry stepped into the barn and shook his head. "You men must've been following Jake for a hell of a long time to know all this."

"No. Our boss is the one who gave him those orders."

"You mean Cumberland?"

"No. Even Mr. Cumberland answers to somebody. Now shut your mouth and check out that stall right there."

Looking at the spot where the gunman was pointing, Harry saw a small horse stall that wasn't big enough for anything larger than a pony. It was the cleanest one of all and looked as though it hadn't been used in months.

"You sure about that?" Harry asked.

With nothing more than a nod from the lead gunman, the others moved forward and swept Harry out of their way. They held their guns at the ready and surrounded the stall before taking a single step inside.

The lead gunman's eyes darted over to a wall next to the stall. When he looked back again, the man was wearing a subtle smile. He holstered his gun, reached out with one hand, and grabbed hold of a pitchfork that had been leaning nearby.

Without a word, the gunman hefted the pitchfork and pointed it at a large bundle of straw in one corner of the stall. Looking at the men standing on either side of him, the gunman waited until he got affirming nods from each of his partners before cocking back his arm and preparing to launch the pitchfork into the straw.

With one straight stab, the pitchfork was delivered into the straw. It landed in something more solid than hay, since it stuck fast and didn't want to come loose. Although the gunman wasn't surprised by finding something under the straw, he did seem confused that he didn't hear so much as a peep coming from under there.

Suddenly, the rumble of quickly approaching hooves thundered through the air. The rest of the gunmen glanced toward the front door of the barn, which was the direction those noises were coming from. Without being told, one of the gunmen ran over to look outside and immediately glanced back over his shoulder.

"Two men are riding straight for us," the other gunman said.

Still holding onto the pitchfork's handle, the first gunman asked, "You recognize either of them?"

"Sure do. Looks like that courier and the other one who was following him into town earlier today."

"Must've been driven out with their tails between their legs. Go on and give them a proper greeting. We've still got some business to take care of here."

The other gunmen headed outside. Before joining them, the one with the pitchfork pulled the tool free and took a look at the iron tines. The smile that had been on his face before only grew when he saw the blood coating one of those tines.

"Come on out," the gunman said. "I know you're there."

Although the straw pile didn't move, he could hear the faintest of whimpers coming from there. Tired of putting off the inevitable, he used the pitchfork to swipe away the straw until he could finally see a single foot protruding from underneath the pile.

"That's a real good hiding spot, kid," the gunman said after pulling away more straw to reveal Dave's face. "But playtime's over. Sorry."

The gunman grabbed the pitchfork in both hands and drew it back for a lunging stab. He stopped short when something caught his eye. "What's that you got in your hands?"

Dave clutched his arms to his chest and curled up into a ball that was even tighter than the one he'd been in before. "These ain't yours. You can't have 'em."

Staring down at the boy, the gunman recognized the edge of the leather bundle and smiled once more. "Where'd you find those?"

But Dave curled up and closed his eyes as if that would make the gunman disappear.

"Doesn't matter, I suppose," the gunman said. "You got what we came for and I intend on getting it. I'll make this quick, boy. You won't feel a thing."

Just as the gunman was about to drive the pitchfork into Dave's chest, one of the floorboards behind him creaked and a single gunshot blasted through the barn.

For a moment, the gunman stood his ground. He didn't move a muscle, but soon his arms were too heavy to hold up any longer. As his head drooped forward, blood trickled from his mouth and then he dropped to the floor to reveal Amelia standing behind him.

"Are you all right?" she asked her brother.

Dave squinted at his sister's hands and groaned, "Hey! That's my gun!"

FORTY-THREE

Even though the gunmen outside heard the shot in the barn, there wasn't much they could do about it. Clint and Jake were already riding straight toward them with their guns drawn. Since it was too late to stop them before their horses got within firing range, the gunmen spread out and sighted down their own barrels.

Clint's gun hand didn't even waver as he drew Eclipse to a halt and took in his surroundings. He could see two men right away, but another two came into sight from behind the Learners' house.

"We heard shooting," Clint said. "What's going on here?"

"Nothing for you to be concerned about," one of the gunmen said. "Go on about your business."

"These folks are friends of mine. That means this is my business."

"We're here to collect something that belongs to us. I wouldn't suggest standing in our way."

Clint had dealt with plenty of hired guns in his life. Some were like the cowboys that had been dogging their trail for most of the time that he'd been riding with Jake. Men like that were out to make some quick money and

174

work up some good stories to pass around their favorite saloon. The men Clint saw now were a whole other breed.

The gunmen standing before him were killers. Their blood ran cold through their veins and their eyes were already dead in their sockets. They worked to earn money, but they also took pride in their work. They were true professionals.

They were the most dangerous kind to carry a gun.

"You were hired by Mr. Cumberland?" Clint asked.

He wasn't surprised when he didn't get an answer to that right away. True professionals didn't toss around that sort of information when it wasn't necessary.

"Whatever you're after," Clint said, "it isn't here. We were just in town talking to Mr. Cumberland and got things squared away with him."

"Nice try," the gunman said. "But we wouldn't be here if that was the case. If you truly do care about the folks that live here, you'd best move along before another one of them gets hurt."

Clint's eyes narrowed. "What do you mean by that?"

"Just what I said. We found one of them in the barn back there. By the sound of it, that one's already been shot. Until we get what we want, they'll keep getting shot until there aren't any left."

"I'd say you fellas aren't completely running this show," Jake said. When he caught Clint's eye, he nodded toward the front of the house and the bodies lying there.

"I saw those, too," Clint added. "And neither of them live here."

"Which is all the more reason why we should get what we're after real quick," the gunman stated. "Seeing as how we're already not in a very good mood."

There was no feeling in the gunman's eyes.

Clint could see plainly enough that he barely even cared about the dead men lying nearby.

That was another reason professionals were so much more dangerous than angry cowboys.

Before anyone could say another word, gunfire crackled from the house and lights flickered in the upstairs windows like a photographer's flash powder. Clint knew better than to take his eyes off of the gunmen for more than a heartbeat, which was how he saw the smug grin form on their faces.

"Sounds like they got another one," the gunman said.

As he stood there, Clint thought back to everything that had brought him to that point. He thought about how careful he'd thought he'd been and how hard he'd tried to keep the Learners safe once he got the first inkling they might be in danger.

For the life of him, he still couldn't see where it all went so wrong.

But there wasn't time to stand around contemplating all of that. Clint and Jake had raced out to the Learner place for one purpose and they still had to finish it up.

"If you're after those papers," Clint said quickly, "you won't find them here. Jake's not stupid enough to let them out of his sight for a moment."

Jake's voice emerged like a creak from the back of his throat. "Actually, that's not quite . . ."

Even though Jake shut himself up before finishing, Clint knew all too well what the rest of those words were going to be. He wasn't the only one to hear them, either, since the gunmen now took a few steps forward to make their presence known.

Those gunmen had Clint and Jake covered on all sides.

FORTY-FOUR

Clint could feel the bad intentions hanging like a thick, pungent fog in the air. It was no longer a question of whether the gunmen would shoot. It was only a matter of when they would start pulling their triggers. Rather than wait for them to work on their own schedule, Clint glanced over to Jake and asked, "You ready?"

Jake's only reply was a slow exhale as he groaned, "Aw, hell."

With those words still hanging in the air, Clint and Jake launched into motion. As Clint snapped up his arm to aim the modified Colt, Jake dropped down to one knee and took a shot from there.

If they'd been caught even slightly off their guard, the gunmen gave no sign. Instead, they held their ground and started taking shots of their own. One of the men dropped with a fresh hole in his chest, delivered from Clint's gun, which didn't even seem to be noticed by the rest of the men, who just moved toward some cover while continuing to fire.

When he saw the barn door swing open to his side, Clint turned to point his Colt in that direction. A split-second before he fired, he saw Amelia standing in the doorway with a pistol in her hand. Rather than say what was on his mind, Clint ran toward the door while Amelia started pulling her trigger to cover him.

Once he was inside, Clint leaned out to fire a few more rounds through the door. "You should be hiding," he said to her. "You're only going to get hurt in this."

Her voice was steady as she replied, "I can take care of myself."

It was right about then that Clint noticed the body lying in the straw. "Yeah. I guess you can. Where are Frank and Dave?"

"Dave's in here and my father is in the house. I wanted to go and help him, but I saw all those men going into the barn where Dave was hiding."

Clint spotted the young man sitting in a nearby stall with his legs stretched out in front of him. One of his legs sported a large, bloody gash. "Don't fret about a thing. You did great. Are you all right, Dave?" Clint asked.

Dave nodded. "I stayed real quiet, but they found me anyways. They never got this from me, though."

Spotting the familiar leather bundle in Dave's grasp, Clint asked, "Where'd you get that?"

"Jake hid it in here. When those men came, I thought I'd better go get it before it got stolen. Pa's always talking about how men from town will steal away anything that ain't nailed down."

"Toss that over here."

Only after a nod from his sister did Dave throw the leather bundle to Clint. As soon as he caught the bundle in his free hand, Clint squeezed his trigger and sent another one of the gunmen outside into the Great Beyond.

Clint ducked into the barn and quickly flipped open the Colt's cylinder. After stuffing the bundle into his jacket pocket, he reloaded his gun with fresh rounds from his belt. "Where the hell is Jake?"

"Right here," Jake said as he rushed in through the back door.

"Why the hell did you leave those papers here? You knew damn well I didn't want to give those assholes any reason to come back here!"

"I made up another bundle that looked just like it," Jake whined. "Put it in the same spot and everything. I don't know how they knew it wasn't the real thing."

"All they had to do was look in the bundle you were carrying and they could have done that any number of times." Clint snapped the cylinder shut and took a quick look outside. The gunmen had already found places to hide rather than stand out in the open.

"I even hid that away real good," Jake continued. "Lord only knows how it was found."

"I'm real good at finding things," Dave said.

"Yeah," Jake grunted. "That's just dandy."

"Well, the three of you stay here," Clint said. "I'm going to the house to see about getting Frank out of there. Do you think you can hold out for a minute or two?"

"Sure," Jake said.

"Actually, I was talking to her."

Without missing a beat, Amelia nodded. "I don't have many bullets left, but I should be all right."

Clint looked at the guns in Jake's and Amelia's hands and said, "Give her some fresh bullets, Jake. I'll be right back."

As he bolted from the barn, Clint pulled the door shut behind him. When he looked back after doing that, he saw one of the gunmen peek out from around the corner. Two shots went off simultaneously and hot lead dug like a claw in Clint's arm. The shot Clint fired did a lot more damage and caught the gunman in the face.

More shots blazed through the air, but Clint could only keep running toward the house, since he couldn't see where the other gunmen were hiding. Somehow, he managed to get into the house before taking anything worse than a scratch.

After taking only a few steps inside, Clint was greeted by the sight of carnage. One body was lying at the top of the stairs. Although he couldn't see any details, Clint could see that another man was up there as well. Clint took the stairs two at a time until he could see the second man lying there.

"Oh, no," Clint said as he dropped to one knee and reached out to Frank. "Say something."

Slowly, Frank's eyes opened a bit and he began to say something. His first words were garbled as blood poured from his mouth. ". . . my fault. I'm . . . sorry."

"No, Frank. It's not your fault."

"Yes it is," the old man insisted. "Just . . . protect . . ." He couldn't get out any more before the rest of his strength left him and the bit of a spark that had been in his eyes was snuffed out.

Clint stood up as he heard steps coming from one of the other bedrooms. A man Clint didn't recognize stepped out of Amelia's room. The moment he spotted Clint, the man brought up the gun he was holding, as his finger started to tense around the trigger.

Clint's arm snapped up in a flicker of motion. Like the crack after a whip had been snapped, the Colt barked once and spat a piece of lead through the air, which caught the gunman right between the eyes.

While that man was falling over, Clint turned to look into Frank's bedroom. Red was laying slumped against the bed. His dead eyes stared at the mess of papers and old photographs that had been dumped onto the floor.

There was a cold knot in Clint's stomach as he left that house.

Stepping out the front door as if he was just out for a walk, he saw one of the gunmen jump out and take a shot at him. Clint didn't even feel concern that he might get hit by that shot. Instead, he simply lifted his own gun and sent the other man to hell.

Jake opened the barn door, raised his gun, and shouted, "Clint, look out!" as he fired a shot.

The bullet hissed well over Clint's head as he twisted around completely and dropped into a one-knee stance. Once Clint got a look at the man who'd been sneaking up behind him, he aimed and fired as if he was simply pointing his finger at his target.

The Colt bucked against Clint's palm and knocked the final gunman over with a smoky payload delivered through the gunman's heart.

Turning around, Clint looked toward the barn and said, "Everybody come with me."

"What about my father?" Amelia asked.

"Just get in the cart. I'll tell you along the way."

FORTY-FIVE

The wagon came to a stop in front of the Bella Donna and Clint rode up alongside it. Amelia and Dave were both red-eyed and had tears streaming down their faces after being told about Frank. Clint gave them a few kind words, patted them on the shoulders, and then climbed down from his saddle.

Mr. Cumberland and one of his well-dressed guards were standing at the front door to the exclusive social club. "You got some gall showing your face around here, Jake."

"Never mind him," Clint said. "Hand over those papers you took."

"Papers?"

"You know the ones I mean. Just hand them over." When he saw the glare on the face of the big guard at Cumberland's side, Clint snarled, "You may have noticed all the others you sent after us are nowhere to be found. Unless you want to join them, I'd suggest you back up a step."

The bigger man did what he was told.

Reluctantly, Cumberland reached into his pocket and removed the papers that had been taken from Jake the last time they were in town. "I hope everyone sees this," he said while handing them over. "I'm practically being robbed right out in the open."

Clint snatched the papers from Cumberland and handed them to Jake. "Yeah. Everyone looks real concerned." To Jake, Clint said, "Get going now and I'll catch up with you, although I suspect we won't have any more trouble. Somehow, I think there's a shortage of hired guns around here."

Jake eagerly took the papers and stuffed them along with the rest. From there, he tipped his hat to the Learners and rode away.

After Jake had gone, Clint shifted his glare to Cumberland and said, "Now hand over your copy of those papers."

"You already took them."

Clint shook his head. "After all that trouble, you wouldn't just hand them over."

"They're the genuine article, I assure you."

"Of course they were. It wouldn't do you any good to give the wrong papers delivered into Sacramento. But you'd have your own copy so you could at least make some extra cash buying up pieces of that land once the railroads start moving in on it. Just hand them over before you join the rest of those killers you sent after me and that family over there."

Cumberland narrowed his eyes as a murderous look filled them. "You'll regret this," he said as he nodded toward the guard, who then removed another folded batch of papers from his own pocket. "My partners won't take kindly to losing out on all that money."

Clint looked at what was written on the paper and nodded. "I'll be sure to tell that to the U.S. marshals when I tell them to come and get you and what's left of your men. The railroads don't take kindly to being swindled either, you know." With that, Clint climbed back into his saddle and led the Learners out of town.

"You think they'll come after us?" Amelia asked.

"There's no need. You and your family were just stuck in the middle of a fight that wasn't even yours. I'm sorry."

"Don't be. You did all you could."

"Here," Clint said as he handed over the copies of the documents he'd taken from Cumberland as well as a roll of bills from his own pocket. "After you bury your father, buy up the land on that list and make a new start for yourselves somewhere else."

"Clint, I couldn't—"

"Just do what I say. I have a feeling that property will be worth more than enough for you to pay me back when I come by to visit you again."

Watch for

LOOSE ENDS

298th novel in the exciting GUNSMITH series
from Jove

Coming in October!

J. R. ROBERTS

THE GUNSMITH

Available wherever books are sold or at
penguin.com